"My letter of resignation is printing now."

"Lizzy, it might take you a year to land a comparable position. Are you prepared to give up everything?" Cameron asked.

"Yes," she said simply.

"Then I hope you've got cable. That's a lot of time to spend alone."

Her fussy movements stilled. "What makes you think I'll be alone?"

"No offense, honey, but your social life isn't exactly active. By choice, I'm sure," he added hastily and much too late.

Ten years she'd waited for him to call her honey, to see his eyes warm with tenderness. But *not* out of pity.

Deep in that place where insecurity and pride waged war in a woman's soul, the latter raised a mighty sword and sounded a Valkyrie battle cry.

Elizabeth lifted her chin. "Please don't worry about me. I won't be alone. Along with finding a new job, I'll be starting a second career. The most exciting and challenging one any woman can have."

"And in plain English that would mean?"

That I'm through settling for what I can get. "It means I'm getting married, Cameron. If you really want what's best for me, you'll wish me well."

Dear Reader,

I've been an executive in a large financial institution, a co-owner of an advertising agency and a novelist. Each career has provided moments of profound satisfaction, tremendous frustration and everything in between. Sound familiar?

Of course it does. I've described the lives of Superromance readers.

Whether you work outside the home or in, own a huge corporation or a mom-and-pop business, you're required to squeeze too many responsibilities into too little time for too little money and too little appreciation. That's not a whine. That's human nature. And life in the world today.

At times, professional goals clash with personal ones, and difficult choices must be made. I hope each and every hardworking one of you enjoys Cameron and Elizabeth's romance and personal journey. As they learn to redefine "success," perhaps you'll be reminded of a truth easily forgotten during hectic stressful days. It comes from a poster hanging in my office, and I share the words with you gladly:

"Happiness is not based on possessions, power or prestige, but on relationships with people we love and respect."

Warmly,

Jan Freed

Jan is a recipient of RT's Reviewer's Choice Award, and a multiple RITA Award nominee. She loves to hear from readers, and invites you to write her at: 1860 FM 359, PMB 206; Richmond, TX, 77469. Or visit her Web site at: www.superauthors.com.

THE
LAST
MAN
IN
TEXAS
Jan
Freed

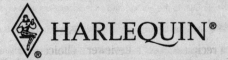

HARLEQUIN®

TORONTO • NEW YORK • LONDON
AMSTERDAM • PARIS • SYDNEY • HAMBURG
STOCKHOLM • ATHENS • TOKYO • MILAN • MADRID
PRAGUE • WARSAW • BUDAPEST • AUCKLAND

ISBN 0-373-70918-8

THE LAST MAN IN TEXAS

Copyright © 2000 by Jan Freed.

This edition published by arrangement with Harlequin Books S.A.

® and TM are trademarks of the publisher. Trademarks indicated with ® are registered in the United States Patent and Trademark Office, the Canadian Trade Marks Office and in other countries.

Visit us at www.eHarlequin.com

Printed in U.S.A.

To Lesa and Steve Moller,
orange-blooded Austinites, master raconteurs
and my favorite twin sister and brother-in-law.
Hook 'em Horns!

CHAPTER ONE

WELL, HELL. He looked more like one of America's Most Wanted Criminals than one of Austin's Ten Most Eligible Bachelors.

Cameron Malloy snapped open the newspaper wider—and *really* wished he hadn't.

Sharp movements, bad! Slow movements, tolerable. Hangover 101 basics a worldly thirty-two-year-old bachelor shouldn't forget.

As pain reverberated inside his skull, he cursed last night's wedding reception. And champagne. The fact that he'd even touched the fizzing stuff, Queen-Mother-of-morning-after headaches, proved he wasn't as unaffected by months of stress as he pretended. Unclenching his molars, he relaxed by degrees.

Okay. The pain was receding. He just might live, after all. Forcing his attention back to the double-page feature article, he concentrated blearily on the other nine photographs. Informal poses all, taken of each interviewed subject ''on the job.'' Not a threatening face among them. At least, not in the escaped convict mug shot sense. He supposed one could argue subtle nuances of definition and make a case against bachelor number two.

The poor schmuck had been caught with his eyes three-quarters closed, transforming his slight smile into a sleazy leer. Less than reassuring in any physician. Downright creepy in a pediatrician.

And bachelor number eight wasn't much better. Behind that startled scarecrow expression, there had to be a brain. The guy was top dog at S-mart Computers, the cutting-edge leader in built-to-order computer hardware manufacturing. Still…he looked like he'd stayed a leee-tle too long in the poppy fields on his way to Oz. Cameron's spirits lifted.

He swiveled toward his desk and reached carefully for his coffee. Maybe he'd overreacted. He did that a lot, according to Lizzy. Taking a sip, he re-studied his own photograph through a mist of rising steam.

His wince had nothing to do with the scalding liquid, and everything to do with his hot-tempered image on the page.

The lens had captured him leaning over Malloy Marketing's conference room table, his braced arms straddling an accordion stack of client billing statements, his murderous expression yelling loud and clear "Get out before I break that camera *and* your nose!"

Damn. Even the lech and dimwit came across better.

Of course, *they* hadn't been ambushed by a sneaky photographer intent on one last "candid" shot. Considering the balance sheet Cameron had reviewed seconds before the shutter clicked, who could blame him for appearing upset?

His office door swung open.

I had to ask.

Letting the newspaper fall to his lap, he braced himself and tried to look healthy.

Elizabeth Richmond, senior vice president and second in command of Malloy Marketing, walked briskly toward his desk, her aura crackling with purpose and the crisp light scent of Lemon Mist body spritz. The fragrance, courtesy of his annual birthday gift, suited her analytical mind, tart humor, and the sweet nature underlying it all. She'd dressed comfortably as well as professionally in one of her usual pantsuits.

This morning's was a dull pin-striped gray. Incongruous next to her mop of curly dark hair, wide-set brown eyes, and Kewpie doll lips. Betty Boop meets G.I. Jane, his youngest brother had once described the woman most men underestimated or overlooked.

For someone who joked his way through life, Jake could be surprisingly perceptive at times.

Cameron watched his colleague sink uninvited

into a guest chair, then mustered his best smile. "Morning, Lizzy. You look extra nice today."

"You look like roadkill."

So much for idle chitchat. "You know," he said dryly, "it's customary to thank a person who compliments you. Maybe even say something nice in return?"

"Okay. I like that navy suit you're wearing. It brings out the lovely shade of red in your eyes."

Jeez.

Her teasing gaze moved to his newspaper and sobered. "Aha. No wonder the aspirin hasn't kicked in, yet. You've seen your Most Eligible Bastard portrait."

Guilt pricked his foul mood. "It wasn't my fault."

"What wasn't? Drinking too much last night, or losing your temper last week?"

"Neither."

"Neither," she repeated, lifting a straight dark brow.

"Yes, Mother Teresa, neither. Do I have to say it again, or is three times the charm?"

She waited just long enough to make him feel three years old. "Charm appears to have deserted you, but I think I've grasped your meaning. You aren't in the least bit responsible for your bloodshot eyes or surly mood this morning, correct?"

Despite the headache intensifying with each second, he suppressed a smile. "And people say you're slow."

"Yes, well—" her mouth twitched "—I have my moments. Next you'll say that Carol tackled you in front of the groom's cake last night and forced free Scotch down your throat."

"Now, now, no need for sarcasm. That's a gross exaggeration." He raised the coffee mug toward his lips. "It wasn't Scotch."

She snorted. "Rum and Coke, then."

Swallowing, he shook his head.

"You mean they served Heineken at a swanky wedding reception?"

Startled, he lowered his forearm and mug to the desk. In all their years of working together, he could count on one hand the number of times she'd attended a business-related social function or client dinner. Yet she'd just named his favorite schmooze booze in order of preference.

"Cameron?"

"Huh? Oh. No, no Heineken."

"Then what *were* you drinking?"

"Ayala shooters."

She blinked. "Gesundheit."

He barked out a laugh, then sandwiched his skull with both hands. Oh, man. Oh, jeeez! Loud noises *bad!* Eyes squeezed shut, he massaged the pain battering his temples.

"Good grief, Cameron, what's *in* an ayala shooter?'' Equal parts fascination and sympathy rang in her tone.

''Poison,'' he said in a near whisper.

''Really?''

Lowering his hands, he cracked open his lids. Sure enough, her distracted expression said she was scanning her encyclopedic memory.

''There's a traditional liquor in Japan that's produced by taking live venomous snakes, mashing them into a fermenting potion, then collecting the runoff. But I don't think it's called ayala....'' Her unfocused gaze lit with triumph and snapped to his. ''Yes, *mam!*''

''Yes, ma'am, what?''

She smiled indulgently. ''*Mam* is the name of the liquor I told you about. Spelled *m-a-m,* shortened from poisonous snakes called *mamushi.* They're indigenous to the Pacific islands, but related to our copperheads in North America. Remember that oral report on Japanese customs that I gave in Mrs. Conner's class?''

Actually, her red-faced stumbling delivery was one of the few things he did remember about Lizzy from their high school days. He struggled for a tactful answer.

Her enthusiasm dimmed. ''Stupid question. It was a long time ago.''

His heart squeezed. ''O-o-oh, yeah, *mamushi.* I remember, now. Crazy party animals, right?''

She looked at him strangely.

"Can't go anywhere without getting smashed," he explained.

Her incredulous groan turned into low laughter, a rich tumble of sound as infectious as it was rare. When her smile faded, the lively light in her eyes had been restored. "Pretty lame, Malloy. Be sure and pass that on to Jake next time he's in town. He'll love it."

Ridiculously pleased with himself, Cameron leaned back in his chair and propped threaded fingers on his stomach. "Why don't you tell him yourself? He's driving up from Lake Kimberly in two weeks for the ADDY Awards, along with Dad and Nancy. Travis and Kara are coming, too. Even Seth said he'll be there."

"Your whole family's going?"

Cameron nodded. After Malloy Marketing had received sixteen award nominations, he'd impulsively invited the entire Malloy clan to attend the ceremony. "You can join our table and make it an even number. C'mon, Lizzy. I'd really like you to attend this year."

Her eyes rounded, then narrowed. "Why?"

Jeez. "We've been nominated for ADDY Awards—what?—ten years now?"

"Eight. The Austin Telco introductory campaign was our first shot at a decent production budget."

So it had been. "Okay, eight. And I've tried to

talk you into going to the awards ceremony eight years in a row without—"

"Five."

At his sharp glance, her chin rose. A tide of pink swept up her pale throat.

"Facts are facts," she said doggedly. "You asked me five years in a row. I'm sure for the past three years you thought, and rightly so, that I didn't want to attend."

In truth, he couldn't remember thinking about her, period.

His foul mood worsened. "The *facts* are that I dress in a monkey suit every year, and eat rubber chicken and smile until my face hurts, and accept insincere congratulations that belong as much to you as to me. You should sit beside me for once and share all the fun, damn it."

"But…what about Carol?"

His mind scrambled for footing.

"You *do* remember Carol? Tall. Gorgeous. Blond. Laughs at everything you say."

And annoyed him more with each successive date. Cameron made a quick decision to break off his relationship with the well-connected social-ite…uh-oh. He vaguely recalled her giggled yes in response to his woozy invitation last night.

Damn, but he hated champagne!

"Not a problem," he hedged. "The table is round. Carol can sit on my other side."

Lizzy's flush reached high tide. "Look, I appreciate the invitation, but you know I hate those stuffy black-tie affairs. I'd much rather stay at home."

An odd urgency compelled him to change her mind. "Why don't you invite your folks to come? They'd enjoy seeing their only daughter pick up a slew of gaudy awards. It'll be a fun evening out for them, and Dad and Nancy would love their company. Besides, with Jerry and Marian sitting at the table, my brothers might actually behave themselves."

Her thick short lashes fluttered and dropped. She tweaked the crease of her slacks. "My mother's name is Muriel."

Real smooth, Malloy.

She lifted a gaze conspicuously devoid of emotion. "She and Dad are in the middle of ugly divorce proceedings, if you'll recall. An evening together would most definitely *not* be fun for them. Or for me."

"Lizzy..." Any excuse sounded weak.

"Don't worry about it, Cameron. You have more important things on your mind than my dysfunctional family."

He frowned at her self-mocking tone. "Anything that upsets you is important to me."

"Let's change the subject, shall we?"

"But I—"

"Please." Settling back in her chair, she dupli-

cated his pose, her thumbs lifting to slowly twirl. "You never answered my original question. What's an ayala shooter?"

He expelled a resigned breath. "French champagne, served in plastic flutes the size of a shot glass."

"I thought you hated champagne."

"I do. But the senator cheaped out and nixed an open bar. No boiled shrimp on ice. No prime rib station. No stuffed mushroom caps." The injustice still rankled. "Since he couldn't disguise his daughter's wedding as a fund-raiser and dip into the campaign till, his guests hacked at cheese balls and drank from plastic glasses. Never mind that their generous donations helped get him elected."

Her thumbs stilled. "So, to get even, you sucked up as much of his expensive French champagne as you could without losing consciousness?"

Damn straight. "After the commercial I wrote and produced for him gratis, he *owed* me."

"Wo-o-ow. You really showed him." This time, her mockery was directed at Cameron. "For someone so smart, you can be so clueless."

She didn't know the half of it.

He tried for a careless shrug. "Hey, I'm the high concept front man. You're the analytical details person."

"Then why do I feel like I'm missing crucial facts? What are you hiding from me, Cameron?"

A trill of alarm zinged up his spine. "Excuse me?"

She leaned forward and gripped the edge of his desk, her intelligent eyes far too probing. "You've been tense and grouchy for months. You've come in with a hangover five out of the last ten workdays. You're wearing a tie right now with a stain on it."

His gaze jerked down to the pricey strip of silk bisecting his torso.

"Lift your hands. It's underneath. See?"

Oh, man. How could he have missed that this morning? "Big deal," he bluffed, resettling his clasped fingers over the offensive sight. "Stains happen."

"Not to your ties, they don't. Or if they do, you don't wear the evidence. You're meticulous about your clothes. You send your blue jeans to the dry cleaners, for heaven's sake!"

He bristled. "Does this vicious attack on my wardrobe have a point?"

"The point is, if you didn't notice a big ol' nasty grease spot on your tie when you dressed this morning, something is distracting or bothering you, big time." She flicked a glance at the newspaper in his lap. "Then there's that photograph."

Normally he appreciated her honesty. Champagne hangovers notwithstanding. "I told you, that wasn't my fault."

She made a disgusted sound.

"For cripe's sake, Lizzy, the guy barged in without knocking and started snapping pictures! He caught me by surprise."

"I'm sure the feeling was mutual. He'd just shot an entire roll of Prince Charming's irresistible grin. That demon frog in the conference room must've freaked him out."

Cameron sat a bit straighter.

"I can't believe the newspaper printed that pose," she muttered. "The first roll of film must've gotten messed up somehow. That's the only explanation…" Trailing off, she eyed him warily. "What?"

"Irresistible, huh?"

For the second time that morning, her cheeks turned conch-shell pink. She flounced back against her chair. "Don't get cocky, Malloy. I was quoting the article, not my opinion. Fortunately, the reporter was a woman, so the interview is slanted in your favor. It might cancel out the damage that portrait did to your Golden Boy reputation."

His glow of pleasure dissipated.

"I'm not a fool, Cameron. I saw the client billing statements in the photograph. Tell me the truth. Is Malloy Marketing in financial trouble?"

Oh, jeez. He'd rather rip out his tongue than admit his error in judgment. Yet he couldn't outright lie. "Yes."

A meteor of shock streaked through her eyes. She opened and closed her mouth.

The sight of Lizzy speechless unnerved him. His guilt swooped back with a vengeance.

"How can that be?" she finally asked. "We're handling almost twice the volume of work we did last year."

"Yeah, but the move to new headquarters alone ate up those profits."

Her stunned gaze turned accusing.

He tossed the newspaper beside his calendar, rose from his chair and walked to the eighteenth-floor corner window he'd paid for dearly. A half mile in the distance, the state capitol's pink granite dome glittered in October's sharp unfiltered sunlight. The sight barely registered.

He knew what she was thinking. Six months ago she'd questioned his decision to double the agency's space and rent, and he'd assured her the company wouldn't be overextended. He sure hadn't *intended* to jeopardize cash flow.

But higher rent was only part of the cost involved. New furniture, leasehold improvements, computer network and server installation, quality art for the walls, upgraded media room equipment, fire code glass lobby doors…one expense had led to another…and another….

It was either go the whole nine yards, or invite clients to his new upscale address only to hack at

cheese balls and drink from plastic glasses. Talk
about tarnishing his winner's image!

He'd had no choice but to overextend.

Still, he wished she'd say something. Anything.
Her silent I-told-you-so added crushing weight to
the burden constricting his chest.

"When—" She stopped and cleared her throat.
"When were you planning to tell me about this
little detail? The day you declared Chapter
Eleven?"

Unconsciously widening his stance, he turned
around. "I didn't want to worry you for nothing.
The check from Austin Telco came in yesterday—
enough to cover overhead for the month. As long
as I keep current clients happy, there's no danger
of the agency folding."

The last ounce of color drained from her cheeks.
"My God…folding? Things are really that bad?"

The company's bottom line gave new meaning
to the phrase "red-hot agency." A detail he would
keep to himself.

She obviously read the truth in his expression.
"Have you gone crazy? You told Mitch just last
week he could order a new color laser. Lowering
debt should be our priority, not adding to it."

The pressure against Cameron's sternum increased. "The old printer broke down every other
day. Even when it did work, the quality was poor.
And the damn thing was so slow it brought pro-

duction to a screeching halt. An upgraded printer will pay for itself in the long run.''

''It's paying the bills right now that I'm worried about.''

''Like I'm not?'' His headache shrieked a painful echo. Yelling, bad. You'd think he'd learn.

He uncurled the fists at his sides and tried again. ''I did what I had to do to bump the agency up to the next level. Malloy Marketing wouldn't have made the first review cut if SkyHawk Airlines' management had toured the old headquarters. They would've pegged the agency as small potatoes and handed their launch budget to some fat Idaho spud.'' Poised to offer service to thirteen major cities throughout the U.S., the new airline carrier would be a highly visible and profitable account for its agency of record.

''Maybe. We'll never know for sure, will we?''

The pain in his chest caught up with his headache and grew agonizing. Failure, very bad.

''Oh, well. What's done is done.'' She straightened her spine and set her jaw. ''I'll need to review the balance sheet and client billing statements as soon as possible.''

Panic clawed at his control.

''If we focus on cost-efficiency and revise our growth strategy, we'll be okay.''

He couldn't think.

''Cameron?''

He couldn't breathe.

"Hey, are you all right?"

"No!" Cameron roared, heaving off his unbearable fear and guilt.

He stalked forward to Lizzy's chair, leaned down and braced a hand on each upholstered arm. "What's this *we* business, huh? I don't see your name on the letterhead, or the bank loan papers, or the building lease agreement, or the payroll checks. It's *my* ass on the signature line. *My* company you're talking about, not cold facts and figures on a page. So listen up, Lizzy, because here's our game plan and I'll only say it once.

"You'll keep hiding from the real world in your nice safe office, converting real marketing problems into theoretical marketing strategies that *other* people will keep presenting and implementing. You'll let *me* keep handling the agency finances, just like always, without your interference. And you'll keep the company's financial status to yourself, because even a hint of trouble would be bad for employee and client morale, wouldn't it? Especially since Malloy Marketing won't fail. I repeat, this company *will not* fail."

The thud in his ears was loud and frantic, dominating all other sensory input. Gradually his heartbeat slowed. The vise squeezing his lungs loosened. He inhaled deeply and detected the scent of lemons. Good Lord!

Cameron stared down at Lizzy in bemusement as her quick warm breaths fanned his skin.

Her uptilted face was in classic kissing position. Automatically he lowered his gaze to her mouth. Small, plump and pretty. Familiar...and yet not. Sampling those cupid-bow lips would be as natural as taking a sip of Heineken.

And as foreign as swallowing a taste of *mam*.

"I believe I grasp your meaning, Cameron. You can move aside, now."

His gaze jerked up to meet wounded Betty Boop eyes. Every malicious word he'd uttered replayed in his head.

He didn't budge. "Lizzy...God, I'm sorry. I didn't mean all that stuff. You know I didn't."

"Oh, I think you did. It might've taken me ten years to figure out, but by George, I've finally 'got' it." Her expression hardened. "This is *your* company, not ours. You'll let me share credit for the agency's awards, but not responsibility for its problems. I shouldn't overstep my bounds, or even leave my office except at your invitation. Because you're the high concept front man, right?"

Damn. "You're twisting my—"

"*I'm* only the back office details person." She overrode his protest, G.I. Jane on a roll. "I'm handy with textbook theories, but have no useful practical experience. I couldn't possibly help you in the real business world. Isn't that right, boss?"

"No! You're way off base. I've been under a lot of pressure, and I took it out on you. That was my temper talking, not me. C'mon, Lizzy, you know how I get. I'm not proud of lashing out when I get mad, but that's the way I am."

"No, Cameron. That's the way you choose to be."

The icy contempt in her voice chilled his blood. He suppressed a shiver of premonition. "Okay, you're right. I should never have blown up in your face. I'm sorry, okay? Tell me what I can do to make you forgive me."

"Move out of my way."

He loosened his grip on the chair arms.

"I need to go type my letter of resignation."

His elbows straightened and locked.

"What's the matter, Cameron? Are those instructions too detailed for you? Well, here's a high concept." She raised her palms and flattened them against his chest, *"I quit!"* she yelled, and gave him a mighty shove.

He staggered backward and hit the edge of his desk, his rump coming down hard.

She erupted from the chair and crossed the carpet so fast a trail of static snapped in her wake.

Dazed, he blinked at the empty doorway, wondering how the situation had escalated so completely out of his control. He'd had many lively debates with his vice president since founding Malloy Marketing, but never a true fight. An *ugly* fight, complete with insults and bruised feelings.

His fault. His goddamn temper's fault. All his life it had spoken before his brain could counsel caution. All his life he'd been forgiven due to a face and abilities he'd been born with, that made others seem to think he was special. A regular Golden Boy. And now, one of Austin's ten most eligible bachelors to boot.

He raised the heels of both palms to his eye sockets and pressed. Yeah, he was a born winner, all right. Everyone thought so. He'd managed for years to scam them all.

All but the one person whose opinion he trusted and respected most.

Lowering his hands, Cameron conceded he'd pushed the boundaries of his friendship with Lizzy to the breaking point. Wounded pride had demanded her dramatic response. She hadn't actually quit, of course. They were a team. A one-two punch. His creative campaigns and her marketing plans had knocked many an agency out of the competition for choice accounts.

Despite his mean-spirited reference to "my company," she knew he appreciated her contributions. Hell, her salary almost matched his, solid proof of how important she was in the food chain. Still, she obviously wanted him to grovel a bit longer.

Cameron slid off the desk, smoothed his trousers and straightened his tie. No problem.

He'd hurt her, and for that, no penance was too harsh. He would give her the pound of flesh she deserved, even though they both knew she had no intention of resigning. Not to be cruel or anything, but…please. Malloy Marketing was her whole life.

Without it, what would she do?

CHAPTER TWO

SHE'D GO TO NEW YORK, that's what she'd do. *Madison Avenue, here I come!*

Elizabeth marched down the long hallway, her vision blurred, her heartbeat loud in her ears.

Ten years she'd given to that man and *his* company. Ten years of blood, sweat and tears to help him fulfill *his* dream. And for *what?*

Had he thanked her for offering to help bail him out of this—or any previous crisis?

No.

Had he appreciated her arriving early and staying late day after day, year after year?

Not hardly.

Did he realize why she'd followed him from high school to the University of Texas, why she'd majored in advertising, why she'd chosen to work at a fledgling agency headed by an inexperienced owner fresh out of college?

He didn't have a clue.

Any more than he knew she'd turned down three lucrative job offers from competing agencies in the past year alone!

"Elizabeth?" a deep voice boomed from an open doorway on her left.

She whizzed past. Tim's complaint du jour about Mitch could hold. Better yet, Cameron could deal with the fueding account executive and art director. After all, they were his problem now.

"Hey, where's the fire?" Susan called from the office on Elizabeth's right.

She sped by without turning her head. One sympathetic look from the agency's media director would turn on the faucet, and she had to stay tough. She had to stay mean.

She had to stay mad.

Firming her trembling lips, she hit the spacious tiled lobby at a near jog. From behind the curved receptionist counter, perpetual phone pressed to her ear, Rachel smiled her dear smile and motioned Elizabeth to come there.

Instantly her nose burned and her throat thickened. She never slowed.

Entering the second hallway, she focused on the fourth doorway up ahead. Almost safe. Just a few more seconds.

"Yo, Elizabeth!" Pete called from her left.

Not my problem, she told herself sternly. He was a copywriter. Let him write an interoffice e-mail if he couldn't ask in person. Cameron was a jerk, but he wasn't a monster. He'd let the man leave early for his son's T-ball game.

The next two offices were blessedly empty.

She veered inside hers, slammed the door and slumped gratefully back against wood. Hallelujah. Peace and quiet. No curious eyes. She was safe at last.

Hiding from the real world in my nice safe office...

Elizabeth's eyes slid closed against the sting of fresh tears. Despite Cameron's intimidating verbal explosions, he wasn't a violent man. His hot temper burned out quickly, leaving him rational and ready to deal with whatever had set him off. She'd grown proficient at dousing many of his flare-ups before they occurred, and failing that, had learned not to take them personally. His anger was usually about small stuff, not worth sweating over in the scheme of life.

But this stuff was big. A huge hot cauldron of seething emotion. Heaven knows how long this stuff had simmered inside Cameron before boiling over and spilling free. Without the added fuel of tremendous stress, he might have kept the lid on his true feelings forever. But he hadn't. Intentionally or not, he hadn't.

Bottom line, she was only another employee to Cameron. One he clearly didn't consider a partner in any way.

She dragged in a shuddering breath and forced her tempestuous emotions to calm. Could she really abandon the agency—or Cameron—during the most serious crisis to date? No one else knew the company's infrastructure or its leader half so well.

He'd been her first market-research study. A high school project she'd updated yearly. Once she'd inoculated herself against his physical beauty, she'd been able to observe him objectively. By now she knew his strengths and weaknesses, his habits and quirks, the name of every revolving-door girlfriend, every Malloy family trait—

He called your mother "Marian" an inner voice jeered. *He didn't remember your parents are getting a divorce!*

Elizabeth flinched, then opened her eyes.

Financial worries could consume a person's thoughts to the exclusion of all else. Her father was a prime example, and she'd forgiven him, hadn't she? Did Cameron deserve any less?

What about you? Don't you deserve more?

Of course she did! But…never again to walk through those lobby doors?

Always to go home to an empty apartment?

But…never again to be called "Lizzy"? Never again to see Cameron's irresistible grin?

Never to be the center in a man's universe? Never to be a wife and mother?

But—

He'll never *love you! Accept that and move on. Do it.*

But—

Do it now, before you get the hots and need estrogen therapy more than sex!

Elizabeth's shoulders sagged. Oh, God, reality sucked.

Pressing a fist between her breasts, she bled for the June wedding that would never be, the golden-haired babies she would never hold, the happily-ever-after she would never live with the man who directed her actions each day, and starred in her dreams more nights than not. When the last fairy-tale hope drained from her heart, she waited, curiously detached.

Nothing. Not even the tiniest blip of life.

So be it.

She lifted her chin and pushed away from the door. It was past time to get a life. Preferably her own, this time.

At her desk, Elizabeth booted up her sleek Macintosh PowerBook computer and glared at the newspaper folded carefully beside her telephone.

"Don't scowl at me," she told bachelor number six. "You'll land on your feet. You always do."

Sniffing, she focused on the screen and composed the most difficult letter of her life. Short, but definitely not sweet. Sweet was the old Elizabeth. The good sport, the team player, the referee and cheerleader rolled into one. The new Elizabeth was head coach of her own game, with her own rules. As of now, Cameron would sit on the bench.

She'd just written "Sincerely" when a soft knock sounded on her door.

"Go away," she ordered, still typing.

Silence, then three sharp raps.

"Not my problem," she yelled louder, saving the document.

The door rattled open. Elizabeth looked up. Cameron stood hesitantly in the threshold.

Maybe it was knowing she wouldn't see that timber wolf stare in the future that weakened her immunity now. Whatever the reason, she desperately needed a booster shot.

The former heartthrob of Lake Kimberly High had matured into a major heart attack.

His extraordinary golden eyes gleamed beneath thick sable lashes, the contrast still as unexpected— the impact still as thrilling—as during her first day in Mrs. Connor's English class. But today he wore expensive designer duds, not hand-me-downs from Travis. Chosen, she suspected, like the agency's decor to show that its owner wasn't "small potatoes"...as if anyone would make that mistake. Whether wearing Armani or Salvation Army, Cameron would exude a confidence impossible to miss. That much, at least, hadn't changed.

But his hair had darkened over the years from sunny blond to antique gold. His jaw had hardened, his shoulders broadened, his legs lengthened, his muscles thickened. He'd reshaped an otherwise classically perfect nose while helping Seth worm a fractious mare. The tiny white scar bisecting one eyebrow was courtesy of Travis. A miscast fishing lure, as she recalled.

Watching him walk to her desk, she admitted the imperfections only enhanced his masculine appeal. The rough edge to his polish turned females of all ages into drooling simpletons.

As he pulled out one of her guest chairs and made himself comfortable, Elizabeth swallowed hard.

I have to stay mad. "What don't you understand about the words 'go away'?"

He tilted his head. "What's 'not your problem'?"

"Anything to do with you, that's what," she lied.

In point of fact, everything about him threatened her future happiness.

His expression shifted into puppy dog contrition. "Aw, Lizzy, don't stay mad. You're the one I count on around here to stay rational and calm."

"A doormat usually does."

"Doormat?" His brows lifted. "You're nobody's doormat. But I did steamroll over you back there in my office. I'm really sorry."

"Yes, you are. A sorry SOB."

He looked startled, but recovered quickly.

"You're right. I deserved that, and more. I was a total jerk. A complete ass. A stupid idiot...you name it. In the past ten minutes, I've run out of foul things to call myself."

"Insensitive moron? Immature hothead? Controlling dictator? Let's not forget compulsive liar—"

"Liar?"

Ah, finally. She couldn't have held out much longer against humbleness. "What else would you call a business owner who, for months, hides his company's true financial status from its highest ranking officer?"

"How about 'thoughtful'?"

She could only gape.

"That's right, thoughtful. You have a ton of pressure on you to develop SkyHawk's marketing plan. I didn't want to add worry to your full plate."

"Bull. You didn't think I could *handle* more stress. After all, I might've jumped out the window of my nice safe office."

He smoothed his tie, a habit signaling either uneasiness or a grope for patience. "Would you please forget the lousy things I said? We're a team. A pretty damn great one, in case you've forgotten what's really important."

She reached for her computer keyboard and pressed a button with flourish. "My letter of resignation is printing out now in the copy room. By noon, the whole agency will know I've quit.''

''Lizzy, Lizzy, Lizzy. You're overreacting.'' His sigh fanned the embers of her anger.

''No. I'm simply acting on what my instincts have told me for years. It's time for me to explore new options and accept new challenges, before I stagnate completely.''

His humoring expression grew strained. ''Then help Malloy Marketing climb out of debt. That's a hell of a new challenge. I promise you won't be bored.''

''I'm sorry, but that's not in my job description even if I still worked here.''

''Je-e-ez,'' he said on a groan, looking away.

Presented with a view of his heartbreaker profile, Elizabeth quickly followed his gaze to the large oil painting he'd purchased for her office. A garden landscape. Peaceful and lovely. So skillfully rendered one could almost smell the lush summer blooms, hear busy insects hum, feel the heat radiate from a wrought iron table and two fan-back chairs in the midday sun. The bucolic scene usually calmed her nerves. Today, it only frayed them more.

Cameron never should've bought the painting, good cause be damned!

Last month he'd passed a UT art student beside Town Lake peddling canvases and a hard-luck story, then wound up funding the kid's books and tuition for the next semester. Thoughtless generosity. Charity should begin at home. Most of his thirty-six loyal employees had families to support, and losing their jobs would be devastating.

"Lizzy?"

She met his gaze and steeled herself when it softened persuasively.

"The last thing I wanted to do was hurt your feelings. I don't know what else to say, except that, deep down in your heart, you know I've always understood and appreciated how important you are to Malloy Marketing."

"And how would I know that, Cameron? I'm not telepathic."

"Telepathic?"

"During the ten years I've worked for you, did you ever once *tell* me I was vital to the agency's success?"

He stiffened. "Of course I did."

She could see he believed his claim. Somehow that made her feel worse.

"Besides," he continued in a wounded tone, "I would think your compensation package speaks for itself."

God, she'd been such a fool. "I rest my case."

"Case?"

"That's right, case. As in, evidence submitted and reviewed."

"Pardon me if I didn't realize I was on trial."

"Actually, the trial is over. I've already reached a verdict." She switched off her computer and leaned back in her chair. "Guilty."

"Guilty?"

"You heard me."

His face might've been carved from granite, but for the telltale tic of a muscle in one cheek. "Mind if I ask of what charge?"

"False advertising."

"*What?*"

The old Elizabeth would've scrambled to defuse his rising temper. "You really should get your hearing checked," the new Elizabeth said.

"Try speaking in English instead of riddles this time."

"Okay. You aren't the man you pretend to be. In other words, Cameron, you're a fraud."

He turned chalky beneath his tan. A dramatic response to her theatrical pronouncement, but not the one she'd expected. Was that fear clouding his eyes?

She studied him closer.

Good grief, it *was* fear! Shockingly vulnerable. Desperately defiant. Why on earth did Cameron feel so threatened? Elizabeth wondered, shaken at her lack of knowledge. She'd never seen the wolf backed into a corner before.

His upper lip curled in a near snarl. "You want to translate that into *plain* English this time?"

She struggled to collect her thoughts. "You've purposely deceived me since college, when you talked me into 'joining' the start-up of a new business on the ground floor level. When it suits your purpose, you're big on the concept of teamwork, and delegating responsibility to the employee trained for the task, and rewarding staff through stock options as well as promotions. The sad thing is, I fell for the whole spiel. I even believed I could one day own a piece of the company, like you implied.

"But that won't ever happen, will it, Cameron? Because in the real world, you can't tolerate sitting back and giving me, or any other staff member, autonomy to make decisions that might affect the future of Malloy Marketing. My title of vice president is mere window dressing."

His relief was obvious, dismissive and insulting. "That's ridiculous. You're the best analytical marketing mind in the business."

"Forgive me if I doubt your sincerity, since you won't let me analyze this company's financial data."

"So analyze it! Hell, review the accounting reports until you go cross-eyed, if that'll make you stop this nonsense about resigning."

Unbelievable. "It won't. I've made my decision. Nothing you can say will change my mind."

He eyed her warily for a long, tense moment. "But…you can't quit."

"Watch me."

A thunderous scowl rolled onto his face and gathered force. "Who will finish the SkyHawk marketing plan?"

And there, at long last, was her true net worth to Cameron. "Farm it out," she said in a dull tone.

"With the final selection meeting four weeks away? Jeez, it would take that long just to get someone else up to speed on the research! You know Ad Ventures will pull out all the stops during their presentation."

"Just like I know *you* will, Cameron. And the selection committee will be dazzled." Unlike some agencies, Malloy Marketing only sent one person to represent the account team in final presentations. Cameron needed no backup. Men responded to his charisma as much as women. It really was true that all the world loved a winner.

"Lizzy, if Malloy Marketing goes in with a half-ass analysis of the airline travel market, we can kiss that account goodbye."

"What's this *we* business? My name's not on the letterhead, remember?"

"Would you forget what I said, goddamn it, and listen to what I'm *saying!*"

"You're the one going deaf, not me. Read… my…lips. You have two weeks to hire my replacement. Unless, of course, you prefer that I leave immediately."

Feigning indifference, she busied herself with straightening the towering contents of her in box.

"Lizzy, *think*. It might take you as long as a year to land a comparable position. Are you honestly prepared to give up a VP title, top salary and cush working conditions on the basis of one stupid fight?"

She thought of the headhunters eager for her call. "Yes."

"Then I hope you've got cable TV. That's a lot of time on your hands to spend alone."

Her fussy movements stilled. "What makes you think I'll be alone?"

"No offense, but your social life isn't exactly active. By choice, I'm sure," he added hastily and much too late. His expression gentled. "I'd worry about you, honey. I only want what's best for you. Won't you please forgive me and stay where you belong?"

Ten years she'd waited for him to call her "honey," to see his eyes warm with tenderness, to hear his voice soften to a bedroom croon. But not out of pity. Oh, God, she couldn't *bear* his pity.

Deep in that place where insecurity and pride

waged war in a woman's soul, the latter raised a mighty sword and sounded a Valkyrie battle cry.

Responding, Elizabeth lifted her chin. "I do forgive you. But you were absolutely right. I have been hiding in my nice safe world—" she lifted a forestalling palm "—no, don't apologize again. And please don't worry about me when I leave Malloy Marketing. There's no need. I won't be alone with my cable channels. Along with finding a new job, I'll be starting a second career. The most exciting and challenging career any woman with no previous experience can have."

"And in plain English that would mean…?"

That I'm through settling for what I can get. That I'm going after what I want. That from this moment on, you're going to see Elizabeth, the woman—not Lizzy, the girl Friday.

"It means that I'm getting married, Cameron. If you really want what's best for me, you'll wish me well."

AT HER POST behind the lobby reception counter, Rachel Rosenfeld punched the last blinking light on the telephone console. "I'm sorry, Mrs. Richmond, but Elizabeth is still unavailable. Would you like me to interrupt her meeting?"

A long-suffering sigh whuffled in Rachel's ear.

"No. Just tell her I called again, and that it's important. You won't forget, now, will you?" Her tone implied that her messages in the past had never been relayed.

Rachel suppressed a peeved sigh of her own. "No, Mrs. Richmond, I won't forget. But if you're worried that I will, she checks her voice mail regularly if you'd like to leave a personal message." Hint, hint.

"Well…" For an amazing few seconds, Elizabeth's mother seemed to consider dipping a toe into the current century. "No, I hate using that thing. The beep always cuts me off before I'm halfway finished. It's so rude."

Rachel mentally counted to five, a trick she'd found useful when dealing with her twelve-year-old son, Ben. "I'll see that Elizabeth gets your message the moment she's free."

"Thank you. I need to talk to her as soon as possible. Tell her I'll be waiting for her call."

Oy! "Yes, I'll tell her. Goodbye, Mrs. Richmond." Rachel hung up before the woman could kvetch some more.

Poor Elizabeth. All she needed now was for her father to call, though he usually waited until after lunch. As the divorce settlement battle between Muriel and Jerry Richmond intensified, they sought Elizabeth's counsel more and more often. The nudnicks had been draining their daughter's reserves of strength and patience for weeks. She must have finally run dry about ten minutes ago.

That's when, according to Tim's panicked news flash, she'd quit her job. Loudly. As in "She yelled like a fishwife." *Elizabeth.* Then she'd stormed past his office, followed minutes later by Cameron, looking meek and worried. Susan and Pete had reported the same *Twilight Zone* sight.

Talk about role reversal. No wonder they'd freaked!

Elizabeth was not only the driving force behind new business acquisition, the lifeblood of the agency, but also a calm buffer between the boss's notorious temper and every *tochus* in the place. Beyond that, she was genuinely loved by everyone, and interested in their personal lives and aspirations…though she shared very little of her own.

Rachel supposed since she'd worked here the longest—seven years and counting—she understood being asked to interpret the high drama. It was no secret she and Elizabeth had become close friends. Rachel's co-workers had wanted reassurance that all would return to normal. Still, she wasn't a mind reader.

A *schlemiel,* yes.

A psychic, no. She couldn't even predict what her husband of fifteen years would do. So why had she told the trio not to worry, that Cameron would smooth things out? What if her instincts were wrong?

Frowning, she recalled Elizabeth whizzing through

the lobby earlier with flushed cheeks and glittering eyes. Eyes that had studiously avoided Rachel's. Eyes that could've been bright with unshed tears as well as fury.

Maybe Elizabeth had truly and finally had it with the brilliant mercurial Cameron Malloy. Maybe the way she looked at him when she thought no one watched—the same way Rabbi Levitz looked at the Torah on Shabbat—didn't mean she secretly loved him. Maybe his gentler temper around her, his use of the pet name "Lizzy" when he thought other employees couldn't hear, wasn't a subconscious response to feelings he wouldn't admit.

And maybe you shouldn't kibitz in their relationship when your own marriage is no rose garden, Rachel Rosenfeld.

The beloved voice had delivered countless tender scoldings and unsolicited advice throughout Rachel's life. Her heart squeezed.

"Mama?" she whispered.

A jangle from her telephone answered. Blushing, she glanced quickly at both hallway entrances to the lobby before picking up on the third ring. She connected a freelance photographer to the art department, dealt with a subsequent incoming call, then sank back in her chair, still embarrassed by her earlier delusion. Mama had died of a stroke three years ago.

Funny, Rachel mused, how her mother's "meddling'' used to make her crazy. Now she'd give anything to soak up all that love and wisdom. She was a schlemiel, all right. Only a fool would fail to treasure loved ones until *after* they were gone.

She ripped off her glasses, gathered a pinch of the broomstick silk draping her thigh and briskly rubbed the lenses. If only she hadn't focused all her energy and attention on Ben's schoolwork, his baseball and swimming, his upcoming Bar Mitzvah celebration—his needs and wants. They'd left her little time for Steven. And in her diligence to be a good mother, she'd neglected to be a good wife. So easy to see in retrospect.

But three months ago, when Steven had moved abruptly out of the house, needing ''time and space to think,'' she'd been as shocked as their sweet little boy.

She'd told no one of their separation. Not even Elizabeth.

Rachel's vigorous rubbing slowed. And now her sweet little boy bristled with hostility. He wasn't so little anymore, either. The last time he'd let her hug him, right after his father moved out, she'd been able to prop her chin on the crown of his shorn black hair. This morning, she'd rushed out of the kitchen as he rushed in, and they'd collided nose-to-nose.

She blinked rapidly and shoved on her glasses. Enough self-pity!

Rising, she put the phones on forward, then grabbed a bulging folder from her desktop. The agency vendor invoices wouldn't file themselves.

The instant she entered the left hallway, her gaze jumped ahead to Elizabeth's office. Pete and Mitch stood eavesdropping shamelessly outside her closed door. At Rachel's sudden appearance, the men snapped to military attention, saw who she was, then resumed their straining cocked-ear poses.

Squelching a powerful desire to join them, she ducked into a large room filled with file cabinets, office supplies and two photocopy machines. What were her co-workers hearing? she wondered. Probably he was talking himself back into Elizabeth's favor. Cameron could charm the coat off a freezing person.

But he was more likely to offer that person the coat off his own back.

Four years ago Steven, a victim of downsizing, had lost his job and insurance coverage for the whole family. Soon afterward Cameron had walked in on Rachel crying because she'd forgotten to re-order nondairy creamer for the coffee room.

Next thing she knew, he'd added not only her, but also Steven and Ben to Malloy Marketing's group insurance policy. It had taken Steven nine demoralizing months to land a comparable management position in the oil industry, and two more for his new insurance coverage to kick in. In the meantime, his emergency appendectomy and Ben's bout with influenza drained Rachel's emotions, but not her family's savings account.

There was much more to Cameron than charisma and a face to die for. He was a mensch. A good man. Though sometimes, like today, he was as big a schlemiel as she'd ever been.

Rachel moved to a long worktable against one wall and laid her folder next to the humming network laser printer. The output tray was full. A paper jam waiting to happen. She snatched up the offending sheets and began slipping each one into wall folders bearing the appropriate employee's name.

Halfway through the stack, she scanned the top page and froze.

So much for her instincts. So much for Cameron's legendary charisma and powers of persuasion. So much for a buffer between his temper and everyone's *tochus*.

Oy!

CHAPTER THREE

CAMERON STARED ACROSS LIZZY'S desk, his mind struggling to process her stunning revelation.

Did not compute.

He must, indeed, be going deaf. "You're *what?*"

A fiery blush belied her frosty glare. "Is my getting married so impossible to fathom?"

Damnation, the woman had a talent for twisting his words! "Did I say that? No, I did not say that."

"Then why are you so shocked? Because my social life is obviously more 'active' than you thought?"

Yes! "No. Will you stop answering your own questions and let me finish?"

She pursed her mouth and examined a short unpolished fingernail.

Now what? "Look, you can't blame me for being surprised. You've never talked much about your personal life. But I figured if you ever got involved with someone, you'd at least tell me."

Her gaze sliced up. "I figured if you ever got interested in my personal life, you'd at least ask questions once in a while."

They exchanged a righteous wounded look.

Cameron rallied first. "I respected your privacy. Besides, I *thought* you were completely committed to your career at Malloy Marketing."

"You know I was. But I also want more from life than a satisfying career. Most people do. At some point in their lives, they want to meet their soul mate, settle down and raise a family. And that includes *men* people, no matter what they say or others think."

She'd found her soul mate?

"Your brother Travis is a perfect example," she continued, warming to the subject. "He's so excited about Kara's pregnancy he's like a little kid waiting to open a present. But when he was single, you told me he never wanted to remarry, much less have children."

"Yeah, but—"

"And look how great your dad is doing? Not so long ago, you worried about him being lonely. You were convinced he would never marry again. Then he fell in love with both Nancy *and* her son, and now they're a happy family."

"True, but—"

"What about Rachel and Steven? Fifteen years, and they're more in love than ever. You can't deny that marriage has changed the lives of a lot of people who are close to you for the better."

"No, but—"

"A husband and wife can form the greatest team of all, Cameron. Haven't you ever wanted, even for a moment, to experience that kind of love and commitment yourself?"

He opened and closed his mouth.

She looked so hopeful, so wistful and innocent, her luminous brown gaze like a child's wishing upon a star. Of course, she hadn't witnessed Travis's bitter divorce, long estrangement from Kara and bruising, bumpy road to remarriage. Or, for that matter, John Malloy's twenty-year mourning period after Cameron's mother lost her long battle with cancer. Their pain had been devastating. And devastatingly painful to watch.

But did he want the kind of blissful marriage his brother and father enjoyed *now?* Sure he did. He'd be a fool not to.

And a bigger fool not to wait until the odds on *having* one were stacked high in his favor.

He managed a credibly careless shrug. "I'm a realist, not an idealist."

"Meaning?"

"Meaning that at my age, it's hard enough to meet attractive and interesting single women. The chances of meeting my one perfect soul mate aren't very good."

Lizzy's eyes dimmed.

He smoothed his tie, struck with the sense that he'd somehow failed her, or himself—or them both.

Before he could analyze his reaction, her eyes re-kindled with a mocking gleam.

"Poor Cameron. Having one foot in the grave must be a tough handicap to meeting women. Then, too, being one of Austin's ten most eligible bach-elors is *such* a turnoff."

Jeez. "All I'm saying is that I don't bet on long shots. It's a documented fact that half of all mar-riages in this country end in divorce."

"Documented?"

Uh-oh. She'd taken on the look of Seth's bird dog sifting through multiple scents in the air.

Cameron saw the exact instant she pinpointed her covey of information, and braced himself for a flurry of facts.

"Actually, the fifty percent divorce rate quoted by the media is wrong. The Census Bureau calcu-lated the marriages and divorces in one year with-out including the fifty-four million marriages al-ready in existence, and—presto! A totally inaccurate, but highly quotable, divorce rate ap-peared in the hat like magic. Lazy journalists all over the country yanked it out with regularity. But when divorces are tracked by the year in which a couple married, the correct rate is closer to between eighteen and twenty-two percent. Not too terrible, really...and I can see that you're fascinated."

He blinked the glaze from his eyes and found hers narrowed. "What? I'm listening."

"Good. Because you need to hear this. The chance of you finding your ideal soul mate would improve considerably if you took more time getting to know a woman. More than *six dates'* worth of time, that is."

Indignation prodded him fully alert. "I've dated women more than six times."

"Cameron, you've dated women more times in the past year alone than the average man does in his entire bachelorhood. I was referring to spending time with *one* woman, not sharing your charms with a harem."

Jeez. "You sound like my brothers."

"Thank you, but flattery won't change the fact that you've never made it to a seventh date with the same woman."

"You're wrong."

"Are you sure about that?"

"Dead sure," he stated, ignoring the red flag waving madly in his brain. "I've been seeing Carol for at least three months."

"Seeing her exclusively?"

Frowning, he backpedaled mentally through a succession of forgettable evenings, only five of which included a giggling blonde.

The flag lowered to half-mast.

"I didn't think so," Lizzy said.

He reached up and yanked the knot of his necktie

looser. "How'd we get so off track, anyway? We were talking about *your* love life, not mine."

"You were talking. Whatever happened to respecting my privacy?"

He'd found out she *had* a love life, that's what happened! She wasn't bluffing about quitting. He was actually going to lose his second in command to some bozo he'd never met!

Shaken, he reached for an acceptable emotion and clung to outrage. "You're a fine one to lecture *me* about keeping financial secrets, Lizzy. When were you planning to tell me you're engaged, huh? After the wedding invitations were mailed?"

"Please lower your voice."

"Or maybe you planned to wait and send me a birth announcement after Junior was born? You know, kill two birds with one postage stamp. Yeah, that sounds more like the Miss Cost-Efficiency I know."

"If you can't discuss this in a civil manner, kindly leave my office."

"It's not your office anymore, is it?"

Her nostrils pinched. She looked away, obviously seeking patience.

Following suit, Cameron focused on the large canvas dominating one wall. He'd paid the artist's hefty asking price, not only to help out a talented student strapped for cash, but also because the garden scene reminded him of Lizzy. Her calming presence, that is. She was the eye of the storm in a swirl of agency activity that, more often than not, reached hurricane force. Not once had the painting's vivid roses ever reminded him of Lizzy's flushed complexion.

Until today.

"You're right," she said, drawing his attention to her icy dignity. "It's not my office, anymore. Goodbye, Cameron. Have a nice life."

"Wait!" he ordered, halting the backward roll of her chair. "Answer my question, first. Why would a woman who's never peeped a single word about having a steady boyfriend suddenly announce she's getting married?"

"Shh!" She flicked an embarrassed glance at the closed door.

But he couldn't seem to control either his volume, or the territorial possessiveness goading him on, preventing him from letting her go with grace. "Why all the secrecy about your soul mate, Lizzy? What are you hiding? Tell me. And while you're at it, explain how you can abandon the company that's built your career just when it needs you most!"

She paled, but thrust out her chin. "How dare you try and make me feel guilty."

"Pardon the hell out of me for thinking loyalty should still count for something these days."

"You're not being fair."

"You think it's fair to drop your little bombshell and leave me to rebuild the SkyHawk marketing plan from scratch? You could at least stay until the presentation. You owe me that much, damn it!"

Lush roses bloomed in her cheeks. "I don't enjoy being manipulated, Cameron."

"And I don't enjoy being betrayed."

"Oh, please. Who's overreacting now? If anything, you betrayed me. I gave one hundred and ten percent of myself to you and this company for very little return on my investment. I needed…" Trailing off, she shook her head, rose from her chair and raised her palms. "Forget it. I don't owe you a thing. Even an explanation."

"Wait!" Desperation harshened his voice. "If this is about owning a piece of the company, let's talk options. I'm willing to negotiate an agreement—"

The smack of her palms on the desk made him jump.

She braced her weight and leaned forward, her eyes spitting bullets. "I meant an *emotional* return on my investment. Don't insult me with an equity offer at this late date. You can't buy back my loyalty. You wouldn't even *want* it back if you weren't so obsessively competitive. No, don't roll your eyes. Admit it. You can't stand to lose, whether it's a game of tennis, or a client's account, or a vice president whose title is mere window dressing.

You've fired plenty of employees over the past ten years, but I'm the first one who's ever quit, aren't I?''

"You tell me. You like to answer your own questions."

The roses darkened a shade. "At least I *ask* questions! I'm not so self-centered I think the world revolves around my problems and needs. I don't think everyone *owes* me their help. I don't charm or manipulate or throw a tantrum to get it. I've worked damn hard for everything I've ever gotten." *Unlike you,* her silent thought rang loud and clear, an echo of her earlier sentiment.

You aren't the man you pretend to be. In other words, Cameron, you're a fraud.

Grimacing, Cameron closed his eyes and massaged his temples. There was enough truth in her accusations to bring his headache back full force. She'd never pulled any punches with him, but he hadn't realized she thought *this* poorly of him. The wonder was that she hadn't resigned sooner.

Then again, she wasn't a quitter by nature, like he was.

"I have some aspirin in my purse," she said brusquely, unable to disguise the worry in her voice. "Why don't you take two more?"

Ah, Lizzy. Sweet, tough Lizzy.

"Thanks," he said without opening his eyes. "But I've already taken about six."

She made a small sound of displeasure. "Last night it was champagne, today it's aspirin…hey, I know. There's some spray adhesive in the art supply closet. Wanna sniff that next?"

One corner of his mouth tipped up.

He opened his eyes. "Nah. I spotted a pan of Rachel's to-die-for blintzes in the coffee room. Figured I'd try to OD on five or six of those rich suckers in a little while." Why French fries would clog his arteries, according to Rachel, but rolled crepes filled with cream cheese wouldn't, only she knew. "Wanna join me?"

Lizzy pressed a hand to her stomach. "Just the thought of two makes me feel queasy. But you go right ahead. I wouldn't want to spoil your food hangover."

Despite the encouraging hint of her smile, she did look a little green at the gills. For the first time, he noticed how physically exhausted she seemed. Those bruised half-moons under her eyes hadn't developed overnight. She'd either been losing sleep consistently, or she'd been ill, or…

A disturbing possibility jarred him.

"Are you pregnant?" he blurted.

Her eyes widened.

A half-dozen emotions bombarded him. His usual glibness fled. "If you are, well…that's great, honey." The careless bozo should be horsewhipped

"I mean, there's nothing for you to be embarrassed about. You're getting married, right?"

A choked sputter escaped her throat.

He scowled. "You *are* getting married?"

Her yelp of laughter turned into a string of violent coughs, punctuated by a final chuckle. "Relax, Pa, I'm not pregnant. You can put away your shotgun now."

Wiping a thumb over water-spiked lashes, she met his gaze. Whatever she saw in his expression killed the last trace of merriment in hers. "I'm sorry for laughing at your concern, Cameron. I'm a little punchy. I haven't been getting much sleep, lately. I've been staying with Mom off and on the past couple of weeks. She has insomnia. The divorce has been pretty rough on her."

"Sounds like it's been no picnic for you, either."

Lizzy shrugged, as if it went without saying any daughter would sacrifice her own sleep in order to comfort her mother.

Humbled, he studied her a long moment. "You're something else. I'm way too late in offering, but is there anything I can do to help you?"

"Yes. Please don't make it harder for me to leave the company than it already is. I care about what happens to Malloy Marketing. You can't possibly doubt that. And I'll complete as much of the SkyHawk marketing plan as possible in the next two weeks. But my priorities have shifted. I want to have a baby. Several babies, if I'm lucky.''

Warmth stirred in his heart and groin simultaneously. Jeez. She wasn't the only one who was punchy.

''I always envied other children who had siblings,'' she confessed. ''Being an only child is a drag.''

He made a face. ''Being one of four brothers can be a real pain in the ass, too.''

''Maybe. But most of the time it's fun. No, I want a big family. And I *am* thirty-one years old. The sooner I get started trying, the better. So…do we have a deal?''

God, he would miss her.

''Deal. I hope your fiancé knows how lucky he is. When do I get to meet him?''

Her gaze veered off to land somewhere over his shoulder. ''Um…soon, I hope. You know, if I'm going to cram four weeks of work into two, I'd better get cracking.''

The red flag in his brain slowly rose. ''A few more minutes won't make a difference. What's his name?''

''Whose name?''

The flag fluttered. ''The man who'll father all those babies you want. The one who offered you 'the most exciting and challenging career any

woman with no previous experience can have.'
That man's name.''

"Oh, you mean Larry." She grabbed the ceramic
mug sitting next to a folded newspaper, then drew
it to her breast like a waif begging for coins. "I
need more coffee."

"Larry," he repeated.

"That's right. Larry. Have you tried to OD on
caffeine, yet? Beats aspirin, hands down. Want me
to bring you a cup?"

"Does he have a last name? Or is he just Larry?
Like Fabio, or Sting?"

She stood. "I'm headed that way. It's really no
trouble—"

"Goddamn it, Lizzy! Do I have to buy a vowel
to fill in the blanks about this guy?" Her cheeks
matched the red flag flapping like hell in Cameron's
brain.

"His name is Larry Sanderson. He's brilliant.
He's kind. And he *never* yells." After a pointed
look, she marched toward the door in a huff.

Larry Sanderson, Larry Sanderson... Cameron
stiffened.

His gaze zeroed in on the folded newspaper, then
flew to the furious woman nearing the door.

"Lizzy, wait!"

She grasped the doorknob and sighed. "What
now?"

"You can't marry the *dimwit*."

Two heartbeats passed.

The stare she directed over her shoulder could've shriveled a grape into a raisin. "Don't worry. There's only one dimwit I can claim to know personally. And I wouldn't marry *you*, Cameron Malloy, if you were the last man in Texas!" With a toss of her dark curls, she flung open the door.

Mitch, Pete and Rachel staggered forward into the room, their heads twisted in identical awkward positions.

Lizzy growled in disgust, shoved her way through the flame-faced group and disappeared from sight.

Cameron leaned back and tapped his chin thoughtfully. He'd been called a lot of things he deserved in his life, but dimwit wasn't one of them.

Something funny was going on. Something besides the Three Stooges currently backing out the door. If his suspicions were true, then his deal with Lizzy was off.

Which meant he still had a chance not to fail.

CHAPTER FOUR

AT SEVEN-THIRTY the next night, Elizabeth drove into the parking garage of Capitol Tower, the high-rise condominiums where Cameron lived, and willed her jittery stomach to calm.

This was insane. She'd known the man since high school, for heaven's sake. There was absolutely no reason for her to be this nervous.

Relaxing her white-knuckle grip, she swung into a visitor's space and cut the engine of her Taurus.

Her heartbeat tripled.

Who was she kidding? She'd known Cameron half her life, true, but she'd never actually *socialized* with him, never sought to be more than his friend and colleague. In high school, the All-State quarterback and senior class president had been hounded by more popular and beautiful girls. When he'd noticed Elizabeth at all, he'd been nice...but he'd been nice to everyone—that was part of his genuine charm. To him, she'd been a studious girl in his English class, as easily forgotten as her stammering oral reports.

In college, she'd gained Cameron's first focused

attention as a fellow team member in an Advertising Campaigns course. They'd carried the other four students on their backs to an A for the term. The beginning of a beautiful relationship, but one that had never ventured outside of classroom or office walls.

Which was why she'd accepted his invitation to grill her a steak dinner tonight.

She had no illusions about his motive. It wasn't, as he wanted her to believe, to kick off their truce and cheer them both up after their unprecedented "fight." And it sure wasn't to get her alone in his bachelor pad and have his way with her—though, with luck, one day soon that's exactly what he'd want.

Unfortunately, what he sought now was uninterrupted privacy to question her about Larry. The steak was a decoy. Cameron was a master at hunting for the Achilles' heel of his opponents, and the instant she'd resigned from Malloy Marketing, she'd joined their ranks.

Elizabeth unbuckled her seat belt shakily. It was his fierce competitiveness, his inability to resist a challenge that had sown the seed of a Valkyrie idea in her mind. For years she'd watched other women try to "snare" the hunter. Of *course* they'd failed. If she could take a lesson from the master and decide that the means justified their happily-ever-after end, her impulsive marriage announcement might be the smartest dumb mistake she'd ever made.

She grabbed her purse and briefcase, slid out of the car, then locked and slammed the door. Hard.

No guts, no glory. Given the slightest indication tonight that her strategy might work, she would step to the front of the class and, for the first time since joining Malloy Marketing, present her own plan…hopefully without stammering. Head held high, Elizabeth marched across the parking garage toward Capitol Tower and her uncertain fate.

Minutes later, after receiving clearance for take-off from the security desk, she rocketed twenty-four stories in a mahogany-paneled elevator so smooth and quiet, she was startled by the soft *ding!* of arrival.

The hushed atmosphere of luxury continued in the small waiting area outside the elevator. Cameron had moved into his condominium about six months ago, but this was her first visit. She consulted a wall plaque and entered one of four hallways.

Underlying the stately quiet, the driving pulse of a bass guitar sounded out of place. The closer she drew to 24C, the louder it got, along with drums, lead guitar and frenzied vocals. Vibrations from the blast of a song she didn't recognize seeped under the door and literally buzzed her feet.

She set her briefcase on the floor, fished a compact from her purse, checked her face in the mirror—and snapped the sight closed. Egad, what a shock! She'd changed outfits a half-dozen times before deciding on rust-brown jeans and a matching lamb's-wool sweater. The rich autumn color had seemed to require more makeup than she normally wore. But cinnamon-red lipstick made her mouth look so…red.

No guts, no glory.

She picked up her briefcase, squared her shoulders, raised her fist and knocked.

Instantly her heartbeat hammered her ribs.

She shouldn't have come here! This was a big mistake. She should've stayed gutless on safe, familiar ground.

Maybe he hadn't heard her knock.

The stereo cut off abruptly. "Hang on," Cameron called, his bass voice vibrating a part of her the music hadn't touched.

This was devious. She wasn't a devious person. She should've stayed guileless and alone.

A dead bolt clicked.

She should've stayed passive.

The door swung open.

She should've stayed pitiful.

Cameron's welcoming smile faltered.

Oh, God, she should've stayed in the lavender outfit!

His gaze swept down her body, came up more

slowly and glowed. "Good evening, Lizzy. You look extra nice tonight."

He'd said much the same thing the day before, but oh, what an exhilarating difference it made to believe him!

"Thank you, Cameron. You look quite… fetching, yourself."

Glancing down, he loosed a bark of laughter, then yanked off the white dish towel tied apron style around his waist. His jeans and black polo shirt appeared fresh from the dry cleaner's bag. Even so, they were a drastic change from business suits.

She tried not to ogle.

"Come on in," he said, stuffing a corner of the towel into his back pocket as he pulled the door open wide.

Elizabeth entered a small enclosed foyer with a hardwood floor, her nose rising with each step, and sniffed appreciatively. "Mmm."

"I hope you're hungry."

"Starving," she admitted, only just then realizing it was true. "What smells so delicious?"

"Could be the mushrooms in wine sauce simmering on the stove. Or the squash casserole in the microwave. Or the chocolate brownies cooling on the counter." He snapped his fingers. "Oh! Did I mention the French bread warming in the oven?"

Elizabeth gaped. "You cooked all that since you got home?"

He rocked smugly back on his heels. "Yep."

"For me?"

"Well, I was kind of hoping I could have some, too, if that's all right."

Her face heated. "I meant, I hadn't expected you to go to so much trouble—I mean, I didn't want you to put yourself out."

"Lizzy, relax. I know what you meant. Cooking is a form of stress relief for me. I do it to unwind, even when I don't have company." He glanced at her briefcase and frowned. "Speaking of relaxing…you can leave *that* thing on the bench. This isn't a working dinner."

Unnerved, Elizabeth deposited the offending article along with her purse on a parson-style bench upholstered in raw black silk. Above it, a huge beveled mirror in a striking mosaic tile frame reflected her flustered expression.

Calm down. He didn't mean this is a date.

The hopeful hum in her body refused to quiet. Whatever else her resignation from Malloy Marketing had failed to accomplish, it had succeeded in shocking Cameron out of complacency. She sensed his sharpened alertness, as if he didn't quite know what to expect from her.

It was a heady feeling for someone used to indifference.

She turned and smiled. ''I know this isn't a 'working' dinner, but surely there's something I can do to help?''

''No, I think I've got everything under control. But you can keep me company on the terrace while I grill the steaks. Follow me. I'll give you the ten-cent tour first. It won't take long.''

He led her into a living area that seemed the size of a basketball court to Elizabeth, an illusion reinforced by the varnished oak floor and soaring vaulted ceiling. Only three pieces of furniture occupied the floor: a black sofa in the same fabric as the entryway bench, a large overstuffed chair in a red-and-black checkerboard print and a big-screen television.

She noted the frenzied images flashing on screen. ''So *that's* what I heard blaring through the door. The MTV channel.''

He looked sheepish. ''Sorry about that. Sound really echoes in here with it being so empty. I'm not letting myself buy anything on credit, so it'll take a while to furnish the place.'' He caught her surprised glance. ''You're not the only one who can be prudent, Lizzy.''

She arched a brow at the mammoth television. ''Your self-restraint is admirable.''

''Hey, do you *see* any JAMO 55 watt rear-channel surround speakers with overload protection?''

Like she'd know what to look for.

"Okay, then," he said as if vindicated. His expansive gesture encompassed a loft on the far left overlooking where they stood, and a kitchen to the right. "This is basically the beginning and end of the tour. After living in matchbox apartments for so long, I wanted a place that didn't make me feel claustrophobic."

Elizabeth swiveled toward the right. Eight bar chairs upholstered in checkerboard fabric surrounded a granite-topped island counter, the only divider between the kitchen and her wide-eyed gaze.

Suspended lamps resembling flying saucers beamed light on red laminate cabinets, sleek black appliances, black granite-topped counters and red porcelain double sinks. Surfaces gleamed or sparkled. Despite the mouthwatering smells proving that he'd cooked, not a single flour fingerprint or mixing bowl defiled the magazine-worthy picture. No surprise there.

Moving her gaze to the place settings laid out on the island counter, she noted cloth napkins, wineglasses and a floating candle centerpiece. Her stomach fluttered with anticipation. *Pitiful woman. This isn't a date.*

"You're awfully quiet," Cameron said. "What are you thinking?"

Composing her expression, she turned to see him

perched casually on one arm of the sofa, watching her reaction.

"I'm thinking I'm a slob and a bad cook and my house is a dump. Thanks for inviting me over and cheering me up."

A corner of his mouth lifted. "I'll take that as a compliment. You had me a little worried."

"Don't be. I assure you I'm thoroughly depressed." She focused behind him on the far side of the room and found herself moving in for a closer inspection.

She'd noticed it earlier, of course. Painted bright red, the wrought iron spiral staircase curling up to the loft was hard to ignore.

Approaching the intricate pattern of intertwined ivy, she reached out and trailed fingertips over the beautiful workmanship. "This is beautiful, Cameron. More like a sculpture than a functional staircase. Did you have it custom-built?"

"No, Kara spotted a guy hauling it off from an estate sale just as she pulled in. She chased him down, got me on her cell phone, and we struck a deal for him to bring it here."

"Kara's got a good eye for design. This draws attention away from the kitchen and visually balances the room."

With a final rub of the cool metal, Elizabeth turned around and scanned the entire condominium, an idea formulating. "You should consider hosting the office Christmas party here. Capitol Tower is centrally located, exclusive, and you've got enough open floor space to handle whatever Mitch comes up with this year.''

Last year at The Banana Tree Restaurant, he'd led a giggling conga line of Malloy Marketing employees from their private room into the cramped main dining area. When the piped-in Brazilian music had abruptly ceased, the line had staggered to a stop and swayed into adjacent tables. Only Rachel's quick thinking prevented disaster, her impromptu rendition of ''Havah Nagilah'' spurring the dancers safely back to their tables.

Elizabeth met Cameron's amused gaze and knew he'd remembered the same scene. ''You wouldn't have to lift a finger. A caterer could do all the work. You could OD on all the prime rib, boiled shrimp on ice and stuffed mushroom caps you could hold. We'd save enough money on the party room rental fee alone to go first-class on the catering.''

''We would, huh?''

''I mean, the agency would.''

His eyes warmed to burnished gold.

A forewarning she ignored in favor of watching straight white teeth flash in a lean bronzed face, transforming mere handsomeness into blazing glamour.

Dazzled and despairing, she wrenched her gaze away before she saw sunspots.

"Well—" slapping his thighs, he recaptured her attention "—I know you're starving, and I hate to keep a woman hungry. Whaddaya say let's get those steaks out of the fridge and onto the grill?"

He stood and waited for her to reach his side before walking with her toward the kitchen. And damn her pathetic hide, she could *not* stop the thrill of hope his simple courtesy produced.

She stole a peek up at his tall form. "So what has Kara picked out for your next purchase?"

"Huh?"

"To fill all this empty floor space. Isn't she helping you decorate?"

"Kara spotted the staircase, yeah. But *I* planned the space build-out and chose everything that's in here." He stroked the island countertop as they passed. "This is one solid piece of granite. Took me days to locate enough from the same quarry to cover it *and* the kitchen counters." He approached the sleek black refrigerator possessively. "Got this baby at an auction on the Internet. Thirty-six-inch side-by-side model, through-the-door water and ice dispenser. One year parts and labor warranty."

Wrenching open the right door, he crouched down, waved her closer and pointed out features. "Adjustable spill-saver glass shelves. Over twenty-five cubic feet of storage space. Good air circulation so mold doesn't set in. Look—" he pulled open a bin filled with vegetables "—this stuff is over a week old, but it's still crisp."

Leaning over his dark blond head, she caught a scrumptious whiff of sandalwood cologne. "Very nice. Obviously you don't need Kara's help on the home front. Sorry if I offended you."

He closed the bin, reached for a plate wrapped in aluminum foil on the lowest shelf. "No problem."

"I guess I didn't realize you were such a…nester."

Hand on the plate, he paused. "A what?" Suspicion laced his voice.

"Maybe a better word is *domestic*."

"Domestic? What the hell does that mean, domestic?"

She bit back a smile. "I believe the Webster's definition that most closely applies is—devoted to home duties and pleasures. That's a compliment, by the way. So few men are…confident enough to express that side of themselves."

His thumb poked suddenly through the stretched foil.

Swallowing her chuckle, she continued in an earnest tone. "You should stop repressing your feminine side at the office, Cameron. Let it all hang out, like you do here at home. Your yin is obviously very talented and deserves to be—oh!" She straightened and scrambled to avoid his rising shoulders, somehow winding up with her back to the open refrigerator, facing corded forearms crossed over a powerful chest. Her eyes widened.

She'd known Cameron kept in shape. But seeing that shape looming close, with nothing but thin black cotton defining his muscular shoulders and bunched biceps, made her a little light-headed. Her gaze drifted to the firm sensual mouth that was as beautifully shaped as the rest of him.

In high school, she'd pressed a pillow to her chaste lips and pretended to kiss that carnal mouth.

"Don't think my yin isn't flattered, Lizzy," Cameron drawled, his expression faintly amused. "But if I let anything hang out, it'll be my yang, thank you very much. So far no one's complained about a lack of talent in that area."

Because she felt weak and female, she jutted her chin. "This from a man with a six-date tolerance ceiling."

He cocked his head and brow. "You wanna run that by me again?"

She already regretted the first run. "It's not important. Whaddaya say we get those steaks on the grill?"

"Whoa-whoa-whoa, back up. What does that crack about a six-date tolerance have to do with complaints about my...talent?" He no longer looked even faintly amused.

Oh, good grief. "If you must know, it means that

if you break off every dating relationship before the physical infatuation fades, you're not likely to hear any complaints, are you? Right about the time a woman starts to learn the important stuff about you, that's when you dump her.''

''Really?'' A dangerous gleam leaped into his eyes. ''You know, Lizzy, you seem awfully interested in my sex life and dating habits. Why is that?''

Her heart lurched. She darted a look from the open refrigerator door blocking her path on the left, to the narrow gap on her right. ''I'm…interested in trends. I've heard you talk about your weekend dates every Monday morning in the coffee room for the past ten years.''

''I don't kiss and tell.'' Truth rang in his hard tone.

Shamed, she forced herself to meet his condemning gaze. ''No, you don't. Pardon me if I made incorrect assumptions about the physical nature of your relationships. You *did* talk about general things, at the urging of whichever man happened to bring in doughnuts. Overnight trip destinations. Sunday morning breakfast menus. Announcements that you didn't wish to speak with Miss So-and-So if she called. I couldn't fail to read the pattern.''

''The pattern being that I dump women before they learn the important stuff about me?''

''Facts are facts.'' The unfamiliar glint in his

tawny eyes made her skittish and flushed and perversely anxious to put more distance between them. She eased to her right.

He unfolded his arms and she stopped, her pulse rate zooming off the charts.

But he only set his hands at his waist.

"Okay, hotshot, you know me better than any other woman. So tell me what important stuff you've learned about me."

She sidled another inch toward more air. He was using all of hers. "We, ah, don't have that kind of relationship. I only know you as my employer. I'm not a good reference. Apples to oranges."

"Humor me. *Pretend* you're an orange."

She'd wasted too many years imagining she could one day be an exotic orange, instead of offering him a bite of everyday apple and risking rejection. "I can't speak for other women. I only know what would be—what *is* important to me in a lasting romantic relationship with a man."

"With Larry," he stated, at last bringing up the subject she'd been dreading.

Nodding, she shrank back from the sudden ferocity in timber wolf eyes.

"By all means, then, let's talk about the dimwit. You didn't fall for his good looks alone. Was it his brilliance, or his kindness, or the fact that he never yells that first made you hear the pitter-patter of little feet in your head?"

He was ridiculing her wish for a large family!

"None of the above, huh? The guy must have a hell of a yang."

Elizabeth flung back her head and glared.

"You obviously wouldn't understand what makes Larry attractive as a potential husband and father. But I'll tell you this, hotshot. It's more than *you* can unzip!"

His eyes narrowed to predatory slits.

Obeying blind instinct, she plunged to her right and gasped, recoiling from the steely arm beneath her breasts and pressing back against the refrigerator's shelves.

"Not so fast," he warned in a silky tone at odds with his glittering gaze. "You can't make another erroneous assumption like that and not let me respond."

"Wh-what do you mean?"

"You have no direct knowledge of what I can or cannot unzip, do you? Therefore you can't say with any degree of confidence that it wouldn't be *more* than enough to make a romantic relationship last."

Cold stale air frosted her back; waves of sandalwood-scented heat blasted her front. Only minutes ago she'd accused him of repressing his feminine side. Suddenly he was Mount Testosterone on the verge of eruption.

"Fine!" she blurted. "You're a stud muffin. You're a virile stallion. You're God's gift to sexually starved women everywhere. Does that soothe your massive ego?"

A lazy curving of his lips answered. "Are you sexually starved, Lizzy?"

She was definitely hot and bothered. The skin of her breasts felt stretched too tight, and burned where his arm had touched. She wasn't a virgin. But she was extremely picky when it came to choosing lovers she didn't love. And the pickings had grown slimmer every year.

"No," she lied with the last bit of breath in her lungs.

"That's good. That's *important.* Because you know how I hate to keep a woman hungry."

The hum in her blood became a static buzz in her head. She'd always enjoyed their verbal sparring. This was verbal foreplay, and it robbed her of all wit.

His lids drooped. He looked at her nose, her hair, her mouth, dragged his gaze slowly back to her eyes. "When do I get to meet the man who wooed you away from Malloy Marketing?"

She was melting in hot gold.

"Lizzy?"

"Hmm?"

"When do I finally get to meet Larry?"

"Sometime after I do, I guess."

His slumberous gaze sharpened. *"What?"*

She snapped out of her dreamy confusion and

jerked her palms from his chest, appalled. Only her resistance to Cameron's overt advances would pose a challenge he couldn't resist.

"You haven't *met* Larry Sanderson?" Cameron asked, taking a step backward. Suppressed triumph gleamed in his eyes.

It probably gleamed in hers, too. She'd decided the means of her plan definitely justified the end result.

"No, I haven't met Larry. *Yet*," she added pointedly.

Cameron reached up and rumpled his hair. "For cripe's sake! Don't any of the lectures you give me apply to you? You haven't dated him once, much less seven times, and you're telling me you want to *marry* this bozo?"

"Apples to oranges. I've done preliminary research—"

"Research? Je-e-ez."

"So far, the facts support that he wants to get married, and will make an excellent husband and father."

"Is that so? What about physical chemistry, hotshot? If it ain't there, it ain't there."

As if she didn't know? She'd kissed pillows, for God's sake! But he'd been anything but indifferent to her moments ago. "That's not a priority for me."

He laughed humorlessly. "I hate to burst your bubble, but it'll be *real* important to Larry."

"That's where you come in." She held his startled gaze. "I can compile and analyze the data, then develop logical strategies. But I need your creative help with the implementation part. Just let me get my briefcase, and I'll explain."

"Why do I think I won't like this?" he asked the ceiling.

She brushed past him and headed for the foyer. "I don't know why you're being so pessimistic. You said yourself we're a great team, right?"

He muttered a curse to her back.

Elizabeth paused, then looked over her shoulder. "It's a win-win proposition, Cameron. You'll get to land the SkyHawk Airlines account—" she smiled brightly "—and I'll get to marry a wonderful man."

CHAPTER FIVE

TWO DAYS LATER, Cameron called a meeting of SkyHawk Airline's agency presentation team for four o'clock. Friday afternoon status reports prevented nasty Monday morning surprises, he'd learned from experience. If a critical task was running too far behind schedule, he could request a little weekend catch-up duty from the appropriate culprit.

He entered the conference room fifteen minutes early and dropped his legal pad, day planner and account file folder at the head of a ten-foot cherry wood table. At the center, sitting on an inlaid rectangle of slate, five goblets and a pitcher filled with ice water awaited any throat that might feel parched. Rachel's doing. Just one of the thoughtful gestures that made her a pleasure to have around.

Staring at condensation beading on Waterford crystal, he thought back to the days of a Rubbermaid plastic pitcher on cracked wood veneer....

He and Lizzy had mapped out Austin Telco's successful launch into the marketplace on that wobbly dinette table. With no technological bells and whistles. No fancy office. Nothing but their ambition and brains, which were a perfect professional match. He'd always found deciphering statistics and trends a tedious bore, but that was her joy and strength. She panicked if asked to concept an ad campaign or sell agency capabilities to skeptical executives, but that was what fired him up. Until recently, he'd assumed she was as happy with the relationship as he was.

Frowning, Cameron settled into a high-back leather chair custom-dyed to match the table's gray-green slate.

The cushions whooshed up that wonderful smell associated with luxury. With comfort. With money. With success.

His stomach cramped into painful knots.

He'd paid for that smell with client money that should have been used to pay off media invoices. So far, the agency's reputation as a growing and profitable company was intact. But he couldn't continue robbing Peter to pay Paul. He desperately needed to generate new revenue. A *lot* of new revenue. A lot of new revenue *fast*.

Nothing less dire could have made him submit to Lizzy's extortion. He needed her help now. Later would be soon enough to deal with the huge void her absence would create in the agency.

The buzz of an intercom interrupted Cameron's strange lethargy.

"Cameron, are you in there yet?"

He turned toward a speaker phone on the wet bar counter. "Yeah, Rachel. What's up?"

"There's a Jennifer Howard holding for you on line one. She said to tell you she was the blonde at Chuy's Restaurant last night wearing a sheer blouse and black bra." Rachel's voice was carefully neutral.

Jeez.

He'd been sitting alone at his usual booth, enjoying his usual "Chuychanga" burrito and beer, when three women in their mid-twenties had suddenly slid onto the opposite bench. They'd recognized him from his "eligible bachelor" photo, and proceeded to force him into vacuous conversation and watch every bite he took. He'd finally packed most of his meal in a "to go" container and hustled home, where he could dribble cheese on his chin in peace.

"Please tell Ms. Howard that I'm unavailable, and will remain unavailable indefinitely."

"Okay, but she'll pump me again for your home phone number. Apparently the operator told her it was unlisted. Do you want me to give it to her this time?"

Good God, no! "I want you to get rid of her permanently however you see fit. And, Rachel?"

"Yes?"

"Don't worry about being polite."

"You're a good boss, Cameron," she said in a heartfelt tone.

Grinning in spite of his tension, he blessed the day Rachel's son had started kindergarten and she'd grown bored enough to apply for the agency's receptionist position. She was funny, a responsible worker, and both poised and personable on the phone. Best of all, she had no professional ambition.

Answering phones and filing kept her busy and in pocket money. She'd made it clear from the first that her primary commitment was to her family, and especially to her child. Her "baby," as she often called Ben.

What was it about children that inspired such devotion and sacrifice? Lizzy wanted a baby so badly, via a conventional marriage rather than adoption or artificial insemination, that she'd turned into someone he hardly knew.

For the hundredth time since the morning she'd quit, he thought of his initial hurt over not knowing about any "fiancé," and her wounded response.

I figured if you ever got interested in my personal life, you'd at least ask questions once in a while.

Like the other ninety-nine times, he postponed examining why he'd been so selfish. The business crisis at hand was his first priority.

The fact remained that he felt like he'd entered some strange parallel universe. Everything appeared normal on the surface, yet was vastly different. Lizzy most of all.

The knots in his stomach twisted.

As archaic, politically incorrect and just plain sneaky as it sounded, she'd written a step-by-step marketing plan targeting Larry Sanderson as her future husband.

Cameron stretched across the table and shakily poured himself a glass of water. As if that weren't bad enough, she'd coerced him into helping her establish a romantic relationship with the guy! The sacrifices he made for his company.

He took a few calming sips, then set his glass on a brass coaster engraved with the agency logo. When the custom-ordered coasters had first arrived, he'd passed them around as proudly as a new papa showing off baby photos....

Cameron instantly rejected the analogy.

Malloy Marketing wasn't his ''baby.'' He hadn't founded a business in response to a ticking biological time clock. He'd created a livelihood that suited his specific talents and desire for independence. Ironically, he now had thirty-six employees depending on *him*. His actions not only affected their futures, but also those of their families.

For that very reason, he'd learned to discourage the buddy-buddy relationships some employers cultivated with their employees.

But Lizzy often passed along tidbits of personal

news she'd gleaned from co-workers. Plus, he'd worked closely with many of them in stressful situations, discovering as much about their characters as their capabilities.

Despite his efforts to maintain emotional distance, he wasn't a robot. God, if he even let himself *think* about the consequences of losing the Sky-Hawk account, he broke into a cold sweat.

He'd had no choice but to sign Lizzy's damn contract. A friggin' *contract!* The insult to injury in this whole mind-boggling scheme.

In return for helping her land four dates with the dimwit—Cameron had negotiated that number down from her original proposal of seven—she would help him land the SkyHawk Airlines account by working right up until Malloy Marketing's presentation.

But, if for some reason other than her own choice, Lizzy *failed* to go on four dates with Larry before the presentation…she would fail to give Cameron the marketing plan he needed to put the ''dog'' in his dog and pony show.

He still couldn't believe her nerve.

Just then Mitch ambled into the conference room, took one look at Cameron's face and stopped. ''Uh-oh. SkyHawk didn't shaft us and go with Ad Ventures, did they?''

''Are you trying to give me heart failure?''

The creative director's worried blue eyes cleared. "Sorry. You looked ready to breathe fire, is all."

He walked forward, laid a sketch pad and folder in front of his usual chair and settled his lanky frame. At age forty-five, Mitch Dansby looked every one of his years, due to a lifetime of chain-smoking, a crinkling smile that came easily and often, and a long ponytail and close-trimmed beard filled with more salt than pepper.

His oldest son was a freshman in college. The other two weren't far behind. The cost of books, tuition and lodging for three kids was a constant source of worry. At last year's Christmas party, his wife Sherry had joked she was tempted to dissolve a sleeping pill in the boys' orange juice on S.A.T. test day.

Casting another speculative glance at Cameron, Mitch frowned. "Elizabeth's still staying until the presentation, isn't she?"

Her announcement yesterday had generated a sort of sad relief from her co-workers.

"She'd better," Cameron said, leaving it at that.

He pulled his pen and legal pad closer and pretended to review his notes for the meeting.

The account team assembling in rapid succession around the table were the agency's key performers. They needed to surpass their previous bests during the weeks ahead.

Tim Reeves, who would be appointed SkyHawk's

account supervisor, was forty-one years old and an excellent communicator, efficient organizer, and anal retentive budget watchdog. He and Mitch epitomized the dichotomy of ''suits'' vs. ''creatives'' that existed in all advertising agencies.

Their bickering drove everyone nuts.

Tim paid child support for two daughters from his first marriage. Eight months ago, his second wife had made him the proud father of a baby boy. She'd promptly quit her lucrative job to be a full-time mom.

Cameron could have throttled her, since her decision had prompted Tim to ask for a raise Malloy Marketing couldn't afford. But what could Cameron do but say yes?

Susan King, agency media director, was a divorced blonde in her mid-thirties with a heart of gold—except when it came to negotiating rates on behalf of Malloy Marketing's clients. Media reps had nicknamed her The Barracuda. She was childless, but supported an addiction to fashionable clothes that were obviously as expensive as they were…bright. Today's hot pink coatdress made Mitch playfully slip on a pair of Oakleys.

Unfazed, she stuck out her tongue.

Joel Simpson, the agency's art director, had grown fed up with an unbreakable glass ceiling at another larger agency. At the ADDY Awards four years ago, he'd approached Cameron, who'd asked

Joel to bring in his portfolio the next day. A winning decision for all concerned—including Joel's wife and three small children.

She'd scaled back to part-time hours as a legal secretary, prompting Joel's request for a raise, which Cameron had also honored.

Pete Wilson, at age twenty-eight, was the youngest copywriter on staff, but by far the most talented. If—no, *when* they landed the SkyHawk account, Cameron intended to give Pete a hefty raise, too, to commiserate with his assignment to the account team. The extra money should help pay for his son's T-ball fees and the new baby due in three months.

It occurred to Cameron that Lizzy had provided most of his information regarding his employees' personal lives. She'd probably never doubted he would sign her damn contract. Too many other lives were affected if he didn't.

Scowling, he checked his watch. She was five minutes late. Almost unheard-of for Lizzy.

But then, a parallel-universe Lizzy had replaced the rational, predictable woman he used to know.

"Elizabeth was on the phone when I passed her office," Mitch volunteered. "She saw me and waved, but she looked distracted."

So now a phone conversation was more important than a staff meeting?

Cameron blew out a disgusted breath. "All right.

Let's get started without her so we have a shot at leaving on time. Susan, I really need those competitives for United and American Airlines before we recommend budget. What are you still lacking?''

Susan flipped over several pages of her legal pad and found the notes she sought. ''I'm missing outdoor expenditures in Dallas and Los Angeles, and a few broadcast figures in Chicago, Albuquerque and Seattle, but the big picture is clear.'' She smiled her barracuda smile. ''If SkyHawk wants a fighting chance at market share, they're going to have to fork up at least thirty million in media dollars to get it.''

''I'm not so sure about that,'' a familiar voice spoke from the doorway.

Cameron's burgeoning grin died. That's not what he wanted to hear.

Lizzy bustled forward toward her empty chair, and though she wore her usual jacketed pantsuit, he couldn't help searching for intriguing feminine curves. He must have seen them at one time or another, but damned if he remembered her filling out anything the way she'd filled out her sweater and jeans two nights ago.

She dropped a bulging accordion file folder on the table, and sent an apologetic smile all around as she sat. ''Sorry I'm late. I was on the phone with Gary Matthews. I couldn't exactly cut him off.''

Cameron stiffened. The sixty-year-old founder of SkyHawk Airlines owned several casinos in Vegas, and was fabulously wealthy, notoriously eccentric, and reputedly very protective of his privacy. Cameron had never met the man.

Tim released a low whistle. "You talked to the Big Kahuna?"

"It's 'Gary' now, to *me*."

Susan's cat-green eyes widened. "You go, girl."

"Very cool." Pete nodded, obviously impressed. "How'd you manage to pull that off?"

"Oh, it was real tough," Lizzy said with mock solemnity. "I had to call SkyHawk Airlines' administrative offices, and ask to speak to him."

Had those copper flecks in her dark brown eyes always danced like that when she was amused? Cameron wondered.

Joel put his forearms on the table and craned to see past Susan. "No joke? He came right on the line?"

"I had to listen to the Beach Boys for a few minutes, but that was no hardship." She looked across the table at Mitch. "Be thinking about a tape they can play for callers who are put on hold. Something entertaining, emphasizing whatever tag line y'all come up with. A lot of people don't like the oldies station."

Nodding, Mitch jotted himself a note.

"So c'mon—" Susan bumped shoulders with Lizzy "—tell us what you and *Gary* talked about."

"A lot of things, actually. Once he warmed up, I had a hard time keeping him on track. I got the feeling Ad Ventures hasn't asked him any questions."

"Gee, I wonder why?" Cameron said, tired of playing the Invisible Man. "Could it possibly be because they assumed the CEO and president of a new airline carrier would be very busy, and that he might get a tad annoyed at answering questions that his staff can handle?"

Her mouth pursed, and despite his irritation, he couldn't help but appreciate the dainty plump shape of her lips.

Frowning, Cameron smoothed his tie. "I've got reams of notes from my conversations with his marketing director and scheduling manager. Jim and Linda are plugged into what Matthews wants from an agency. Why didn't you ask me before you went over their heads?"

"Would you have let me make the call?"

Cameron glowered.

She smiled sweetly. "That's why I didn't ask."

Suppressed snickers from the others rubbed salt in his wound.

Her expression grew serious. "I wasn't interested in what his staff thinks he wants from an agency. I wanted to know what his vision is for SkyHawk

Airlines. We're all so anxious to get this account, we're in danger of forgetting a basic rule.'' She held his gaze. ''Our recommendations should always stem from what's best for a client's business, not from what the client expects or wants to hear. Or what he can bear to hear without flinching at the cost.''

She referred to the thirty-million-dollar media budget Susan had mentioned. The agency's fifteen percent commission on that alone would cover his debts and leave a fat security cushion.

Beneath her steady gaze, he relented. ''You're right. I'm sorry I jumped down your throat without hearing you out. I really am interested in what he told you. Why don't you give us a summary?''

Warmed by the approval softening her eyes, he barely heard her account of Matthews's ideal airline carrier. His thoughts turned back to the moment he couldn't seem to forget, when the parallel universe he'd entered had *really* turned weird. He'd actually trapped Lizzy against his refrigerator and almost fed her more than dinner. As if she were just another date who looked hungry for his kiss, instead of the only woman who ever looked at the man he was inside—faults and all.

Lizzy provided counsel untainted by fear of reprisal or desire for his favor. She pierced his creative ego when it overinflated, and prevented his hotheaded impulses from becoming irreversible actions. If she laughed, he knew he'd been truly funny. And if she praised...

Ah, when Lizzy gave him a compliment, he could conquer the world!

He was very glad he'd resisted temptation. Kissing her would've changed the dynamics of their relationship. He needed her blunt honesty these next few critical weeks more than ever before.

As much as he hated her plan to catch a man and get hitched, he would honor his part of the contract so she would honor hers, and hope she would come to her senses soon.

"...what do you think, Cameron?" Lizzy asked.

His gaze jerked up guiltily.

Jeez. He didn't have a clue what she'd been talking about, but he did know one thing.

He'd better get over this damn fascination with her mouth soon, or they'd both be in big trouble.

SATURDAY MORNING, Elizabeth rounded the corner of Jackrabbit Lane at a fast jog, surged up the street she'd dubbed Death Hill, and shifted into a zone she'd experienced a mere handful of times.

She was strong. She was invincible. She was Warrior Woman attacking the steep incline with powerful, effortless strides.

The tortuous homestretch of her three-mile route was no match for her this glorious October morning. The second cool front of the season had swept through Austin overnight, dropping temperatures from the eighties to the high sixties. Body, mind and spirit were equally pumped on tangy air, sharp blue sky, and one repetitive thought: *Cameron is coming! Cameron is coming! Cameron is coming!*

She reached the top of the hill at a dead run and passed the street lamp serving as her finish line. Slowing gradually to a stop, she thrust victorious fists above her head.

Pain slammed into her body.

Black dizziness swamped her mind.

Her spirit sank to her stomach, then threatened to resurface along with her bagel and cream cheese. Gripping her bare knees, she dragged in great searing gulps of air. Rivulets of sweat became rivers. Her thigh muscles twitched, her calf muscles cramped. She thought longingly of her house three blocks ahead, where she could collapse on a soft bed.

No, stupid. Cameron is coming.

Before signing her contract, he'd stipulated that they couldn't work on her personal project during regular business hours. They'd made plans to collaborate at her house this morning.

The blackness was fading. She could see her Nikes now, but was still too close to barfing on them for comfort. Warrior Woman—ha! More like Wimp Woman. *Stupid* Wimp Woman.

Three years ago she hadn't been able to *walk* up

Death Hill without almost dying. A fast jog was plenty fast enough to maintain the fitness she'd worked so hard to achieve.

"Elizabeth?" a reedy voice called from someplace close. "Are you sick, dear?"

Elizabeth turned her head to the right.

Mrs. Doppler, wearing a knee-length white robe over an ankle-length pink nightgown, stood on the sidewalk spraying rosebushes planted in a narrow curbside bed. With her scalp showing pink through sparse silver hair, and her head nodding from age and last year's stroke, the eighty-two-year-old eccentric looked a bit like one of her swaying white roses tinged with pink.

One lime-green garden glove shaded her worried eyes. The other wielded a wand sprayer attached to a pump canister. She cut off the mist of insecticide and lowered her free hand.

"I'm okay," Elizabeth said, straightening. "I just needed to catch my breath."

"Well, I'm not surprised. The way you came flying up over that hill, I thought maybe a rabid dog was after you. You scared the life out of me!" A remnant of fear edged the widow's voice.

She clung fiercely to her independence, despite her deteriorating health and a daughter and son-in-law who urged her to live with them.

"Sorry, Mrs. Doppler. I guess I was feeling my oats in this cooler weather. Isn't it a beautiful morning?'' Lifting her face to the sun, Elizabeth inhaled the pungent scents of mesquite wood smoke, juniper trees and insecticide.

"Thomas used to get frisky, too, when the temperature dropped. Ah, to be young again."

Elizabeth eyed the heavy-looking canister sitting beside matted blue bedroom slippers. "Age hasn't slowed you down one bit, that I can see. Why didn't you wait for Miguel to help you spray this morning?"

"His mother called earlier. He hurt his ankle in last night's football game, poor boy. If I don't take care of these aphids now, there won't be a leaf left by next Saturday."

Elizabeth thought of the hybrid tea roses lining the backyard fence. "Are you almost finished?"

"Oh, no, dear. I started on the front beds first. That way if I get tired...well, these bushes are so *visible* from the street." The irony of working in her nightgown to make sure a passersby couldn't criticize her leaf drop seemed to escape Mrs. Doppler.

Suppressing a sigh, Elizabeth walked around the narrow bed to the sidewalk. "Tell you what. If you'll make me a tall glass of iced tea, I'll take over the spraying for a while. I know it's an imposition, but would you mind?"

For a long moment, resistance gleamed in shrewd gray eyes. Elizabeth suddenly wished that her fifty-five-year-old healthy mother possessed half as much strength and pride as this frail old woman in her flapping nightgown.

"I'm really thirsty," Elizabeth added quietly.

Resistance drained, leaving resigned gratitude. Mrs. Doppler handed over the spray attachment. "Would you like lemon, or lime? I have both."

"Lime would be perfect, thanks."

"No, dear. Thank *you*." With a bittersweet smile, Mrs. Doppler turned and shuffled toward her front door.

Twenty-five minutes later, Elizabeth's respect for the thriving garden had risen, along with her anxiety over passing time. She rinsed out and stored the pump sprayer, thanked her elderly friend for the iced tea and finally headed home. A hot shower sounded heavenly.

Shivering in the cool breeze, she glanced at her watch. Five after ten. Cameron was due at ten-thirty. Fortunately he was always late. She'd have enough time to wash her hair and slap on a little makeup before he arrived to "coach" her for tomorrow.

Her research on Larry Sanderson had turned up several pleasant surprises. For a spontaneous selection, bachelor number eight was proving to be far more appealing—on paper—than she'd dared hope to discover.

He was dedicated to his company, yes, but not

to the exclusion of outside interests. One of those interests was Pet Partners, a nonprofit organization devoted to matching unwanted, abandoned or problem pets with new loving owners.

S-mart Computers was the co-sponsor with KVUE-TV of tomorrow's annual Pet Partners Placement Day at Zilker Park. Larry would be there in a volunteer capacity, and she'd chosen the casual venue as the perfect place to meet her future "fiancé" and wangle a first date. With Cameron's help, of course.

Who better to advise her on how to attract a sought-after eligible bachelor, than the most desirable confirmed bachelor of them all?

CHAPTER SIX

PARKED IN LIZZY'S DRIVEWAY, Cameron drummed his fingertips on the steering wheel of his Jaguar. She wasn't home.

When his Saturday morning tennis buddy had stood him up earlier this morning, he'd tried to recruit another player without success. Deciding that the sooner he got his stupid session with Lizzy over with, the better, he'd called her from his car phone and gotten her answering machine.

At the time, he'd assumed she must be in the shower or out running a quick errand. But since arriving, he'd knocked, rung the doorbell, peered through the garage door window at her car and checked her empty backyard. He didn't know why he'd expected her to be eagerly awaiting his arrival.

Or why he was so disappointed that she wasn't.

Frowning, he conducted another 180-degree visual scan of her neighborhood from inside his car.

Massive oak and juniper trees dwarfed modest one-story houses, most in need of repair or paint. He counted four old-model pickup trucks, two battered motor homes and a Harley-Davidson parked within sight. Scattered newspapers on both sides of the street awaited late sleepers.

In the front yard two houses away, a lanky Hispanic teenager stood balanced on his right foot, his left wrapped in an Ace bandage, and threw the last of five footballs at a basketball-size hole cut in a sheet of plywood. Then he bent down, picked up his crutches and maneuvered awkwardly over the grass to retrieve the balls.

Cameron estimated the kid was about seven-for-twelve since he'd been keeping track. Not bad, all things considered.

His gaze returned to Lizzy's dazzling white clapboard house and lingered. The garage door and window shutters were painted slate-blue. Terra-cotta pots of red geraniums and frothy ferns filled one corner of the small front porch. A trimmed hedge fronted by purple, white and yellow pansies hugged the length of the house. Limestone rocks native to central Texas bordered the mulched bed and cement porch.

The entire effect was cozy and welcoming. It suited a woman who wanted babies more than a career.

Narrowing his eyes, he drummed his fingertips. As rich as Sanderson was, if he actually fell for Lizzy, he would yank her out of this house pronto. The neighborhood wasn't seedy, Cameron admitted, but he sure wouldn't want any woman of *his* living here alone. The tall pear-shaped cedar bush next to Lizzy's garage would be perfect cover for any creep waiting to slip inside before the door came down.

He shifted uncomfortably. All those nights she'd worked until after dark, she'd come home and been extremely vulnerable. He would have known that had he eyeballed the property even once during the three years she'd lived here. She'd invited him and other staff members to her house on several occasions, but he'd always declined because of previous commitments.

Jeez, he'd been selfish! The question was...why?

He pushed aside his plaguing guilt. Once his company was back in the game, he would devote energy to retaining the team's top player and free agent.

Scowling, Cameron blew out a breath and checked his watch. Ten after ten. He had twenty minutes to go before he could even start to get irritated. Or worried...

What if she was inside, physically *unable* to answer her phone or doorbell.

He was out of the Jag and halfway to the small porch when his heightened sense of awareness prickled.

Turning, he looked beyond the football thrower at a woman on the sidewalk striding their way. Curly dark hair. Medium height. It had to be...it *was* Lizzy. An alternate-universe Lizzy wearing electric-blue jogging shorts, a cropped white T-shirt and running shoes.

Whoa!

Walking forward, he stared at the woman he'd only seen dressed in pants or modest skirts for most of the past ten years.

Her legs were great.

Hell, better than great. Maybe even spectacular. Longer than he'd thought. Slim, but shapely, their pale gold color so flawless he wondered if her skin felt as smooth as it looked. Lizzy had never struck him as the athletic type, but obviously she jogged on a regular basis. Lithe muscles flexed with every step she took. Strong…rhythmic…sexy.

Damn.

Wrenching his gaze upward, he cataloged other surprises.

She'd sweat recently. A lot, from the looks of her soaked T-shirt and matted wet curls. White cotton clung to her torso, delineating a sports bra and evidence that the cool breeze had given her a chill.

Double damn.

He slowed to a stop on the sidewalk and waited while she closed the last ten yards between them, her expression dismayed.

"You're early," she accused. "You're *never* early." She reached up and finger-combed her hair, exposing intriguing glimpses of flat stomach the color of ivory.

She must wear a one-piece swimsuit.

Her scent wafted toward him, a mixture of lemon spritz, musky woman and…what *was* that? He inhaled deeply, his nostrils flaring, his head swimming.

Lowering her hand, she blushed. "Oh, God, I smell like insecticide. I think I got as much on me as I did Mrs. Doppler's rosebushes…let me run and take a quick shower."

"Who's Mrs. Doppler?"

"An eighty-two-year-old sweetie about three blocks away. She was out front with this big heavy canister, and I couldn't just let her lug it around by herself."

He tried to imagine Carol, or any other woman he'd dated, stopping to help an old woman spray her rosebushes. The image wouldn't materialize.

Lizzy cocked her head. "Would you like to come inside and have a cup of coffee while you wait? You don't have to. I mean, it's such nice weather, you can stay out here if you want." Her gaze shot to the right and flooded with relief. "Oh, good! There's someone I want you to meet."

She grabbed Cameron's arm and pulled him onto the adjacent yard toward the teen they both appeared to have forgotten was there.

He stood hunched over his crutches, wearing voluminous denim shorts that reached midcalf, a Rollin' Hard T-shirt, and one Adidas shoe the approximate size of Travis's bass fishing boat. Five footballs were lined up in a row on the grass within easy reach.

Cameron endured the teen's slightly sneering examination of his navy cable-knit sweater, khaki pants and suede leather Rockports without offense. He'd invaded the kid's turf—driving a Jag and dressed like a J. Crew catalog model, no less. What else could he expect?

The coffee-brown gaze moved to Lizzy and warmed considerably. To the teen's credit, his focus stayed above her neck.

She made a crooning sound of sympathy. "Oh, Miguel, I heard about your ankle. Is it serious?"

"Nah. Just a mild sprain. If I stay off it a couple of days, I should be able to play in next week's game."

"That's wonderful! For you *and* the Fighting Trojans." Beaming, she performed introductions. "Cameron, I'd like you to meet my neighbor, Miguel Diaz."

The name seemed familiar....

"Miguel, this is Cameron Malloy, my boss and the owner of Malloy Marketing."

Somebody had taught Miguel manners. Straightening to his full height of about six feet, he propped his right crutch against his hip and extended a long-fingered hand.

Simultaneously Cameron remembered the *Austin American Statesman*'s sports page article touting that talented hand.

He moved forward to exchange a firm shake. "You're the quarterback responsible for Harris High School changing to a passing offense for the first time in seven years, right?"

Miguel seemed startled, then flattered. "We've got two wide receivers who made All City last year. Our whole offense is strong."

Miguel rose a few notches in Cameron's estimation.

"You know, Miguel," Lizzy jumped in. "You and Cameron have a lot in common. He was only a junior in high school, just like you, when he made varsity starting quarterback. Lake Kimberly High School won back-to-back state championships because of his rocket passing arm."

At the pride in her voice, Cameron's heart lilted.

For the first time, Miguel eyed Cameron as if truly impressed. "Back-to-back, huh? You must've been recruited by all the college big guns."

"A few."

"More than a few," Lizzy corrected. "He had coaches and alumni from all over the country promising him the world. The hottest topic in the *Lake*

Kimberly Journal for months was where he would commit to play.''

''Yeah? Who'd you pick?'' Manuel asked.

Cameron's heartbeat slowed in dread. ''Malloys have deep roots in Texas. I wasn't about to be the first to switch loyalty. A&M and UT offered me full scholarships—'' he forced a smile ''—but the Corps couldn't compete with topless coeds at Barton Springs.''

Miguel grinned his agreement, displaying white teeth and a dimple the media would love during interviews. ''I've been watching Longhorn games since I was a little kid. Maybe I saw you play.''

'''Fraid not. I tore up my knee pretty badly in preseason practice my freshman year. After surgery and rehab…'' Jeez. You'd think this would get easier. ''Well, let's just say that my focus changed. I concentrated on getting a degree.''

Miguel looked embarrassed. ''That's rough, man.''

Cameron could tell that the teen thought he hadn't been able to cut it as a quarterback, but let the assumption slide.

''Shit happens. You adjust, or live with stink the rest of your life. That sprained ankle of yours might be the worst injury you ever have. Or you might tear a ligament tomorrow.'' He hated preying on an athlete's worst fear, but Lizzy obviously liked this kid. ''If you're half as smart as your coach says you are, you'll work as hard in the classroom as you do on the field. Then you'll have options no matter what happens.'' His father's favorite lecture.

From the bored expression Miguel tried to hide, the advice had as much impact on him as it had had on Cameron at the same age. God, had he ever been that young and immortal?

He moved to the nearest football lying on the grass. ''Hey? You wanna pass to a target that can throw the ball back for a change?''

Miguel brightened. ''You mean it?''

Cameron scooped up the ball, positioned his fingers on the laces and backpedaled as if searching for an open receiver. ''I'll give you twenty throws. Then you should get that ankle propped on a pillow, where I'm sure the team trainer told you to leave it.''

Miguel's sheepish expression confirmed Cameron's suspicion. He glanced at Lizzy and paused.

She reminded him of an anxious mother wondering if she could safely sneak away from her baby-sitter and child. Exactly which role she'd slotted him in was a mystery, though.

''Go on,'' he ordered. ''Take a shower before you get toxic poisoning. I'll knock on your door at ten-thirty.''

She hesitated.

He made a shooing motion. ''Go.''

''Okay...if you're sure. Have fun.'' Three steps later she turned around and walked backward. ''But *be careful*. Miguel, don't let him get hurt trying to show off.''

Mystery solved.

Football tucked under one arm, Cameron set his opposite hand at his waist. ''He's on crutches, Lizzy. Just how out of shape do you think I am?''

The look she slanted up through her lashes went a long way toward mollifying his ego. Smiling, she pirouetted and walked off toward her house. *Damn.*

The back view of her legs lived up to the front, and got better the higher his gaze rose.

''Hey, boss man?''

''Hmm?'' She'd reached her front porch.

''You gonna stare at her ass all day, or throw the football?''

Cameron turned to face the teen's knowing smirk. ''It's a pretty great ass. And I've never seen it in skimpy blue jogging shorts before. Gimme a break.''

Miguel broke into a grin. ''You should see it in skimpy red shorts. She has a hot-pink pair, too. And sometimes she wears this tight little tank top that shows her—'' *Smack!*

The football hitting Miguel's sternum drove him back a wobbling step.

''He-ey!'' he protested, repositioning his crutches.

I still got it, Cameron thought with satisfaction. "Sorry, Diaz. I'll go easy on you from now on."

"That's good, Malloy. I wouldn't want you to hurt yourself because of one lucky throw. Elizabeth would kill me."

"Lucky?" Holding Miguel's gaze, Cameron recognized a kindred competitive gleam. "Want me to nail you again?"

"It wouldn't prove much from this distance. Bet you can't drill a ball through there more than once," Miguel taunted, nodding at the plywood target twenty-five yards away.

Ignoring the challenge was unthinkable.

"Five bucks says I can."

"You're on."

Cameron moved to the four remaining footballs lined in a row on the grass.

In one fluid movement he picked the first one up, angled his body toward the target, cocked back his arm and fired a rocket spiral through the hole. Without giving himself time to think, he repeated the action a second, third and fourth time in rapid succession.

Adrenaline still pumping, he was headed for the fifth ball, the one that had bounced off Miguel's chest, when an aluminum crutch suddenly stretched out to block Cameron's path.

"Okay, man, you proved your point."

"Which was?"

"You can throw friggin' bullets and hit the bull's-eye every time." Genuine respect laced Miguel's voice.

"So?"

"So your first throw wasn't lucky."

"And?"

"Damn!" Miguel withdrew his crutch and planted it hard in the grass. "I lost and you won, Malloy. What more do you want?"

Relaxing, Cameron reached over and clapped the teen's shoulder. "Not a thing, kid, not a thing. Keep your money. Let's play some ball."

"WHAT'S WRONG WITH THIS sweatshirt? I think it's perfect for tomorrow." Standing next to an antique steamer trunk doubling as a coffee table, Lizzy wore relaxed-fit jeans, a mutinous scowl and a large gray sweatshirt she'd wangled from the agency's KVUE-TV rep.

Cameron lifted his arm to the back of her living room sofa and battled an irrational desire to let her wear the damn thing.

Unfortunately, if he expected to fulfill her contract, she needed to hear the unvarnished truth. But where to begin?

At the tacky red logos of Pet Partners, S-mart Computers and Channel 24 embroidered over her heart? Or the camouflaging coverage from her neck to the top of her thighs? Or the blah gray fleece making her brunette coloring look washed-out and dull?

"Well?" she demanded.

He glanced down at Roman numeral III of the marketing plan in his lap. "Look, you're the one who listed 'wardrobe' under Competitive Weaknesses, not me. What good is acknowledging a weakness, if you're not receptive to change?"

Ever logical, she conceded his point with a grudging nod. "All right, go on."

"First off, sweatshirts scream suburban housewife. Sanderson will look right past you and notice women dressed for the hunt."

"I'm dressing for a day at the park, remember?"

"You're dressing for Sanderson," he corrected in a hard voice.

"Okay, that, too. And I think he'll notice his company logo right away, and it will set me apart from most of the women there."

"Not embroidered on that baggy thing, it won't."

"Sweatshirts are *supposed* to be baggy and comfortable."

"You want comfort? Wait'll you've had four dates with the guy. Until then, show 'im the merchandise, baby."

"*What?*"

"Don't be coy. Or hypocritical. You did your consumer research and selected the product you want to buy—namely Larry Sanderson. Now you want one of Austin's ten most eligible bachelors to reach specifically for you among a shelf full of brands screaming Single Hot Babe, Satisfaction Guaranteed! Do you honestly think his company logo can compete against that message?''

Her outraged expression neutralized. She sat slowly on one corner of the steamer trunk, her battered Nikes six inches from his Rockports, and clasped her hands. ''All right, go on.''

''What's the first rule of packaging, Lizzy?''

''Attract attention,'' she admitted, her mouth thinning. ''So you're saying that this MIT graduate, a man who founded and runs a company getting a 160 percent annual return on invested capital, is not smart enough to look inside the package?''

''No. I'm saying he's a guy. And under normal circumstances, guys don't look inside the package unless their hormones first motivate them to pick it up. Brains kick in later.''

''You're confirming the male pig stereotype. I happen to think Larry is much more emotionally mature than that.''

Larry, was it? Jeez. ''Based on what?''

''His involvement with Pet Partners, for one thing. He could've simply donated money for the tax write-off and left it at that. Larry has been an active spokesperson for the organization within the business community. He logs in at least sixteen volunteer hours a month at the shelter. The director said he cleans kennels and gives flea baths same as everybody else.''

''That makes him an animal lover, not mature.''

''That makes him humble and unselfish, which is a good indication that he's also mature.''

Bully for Saint Larry.

''Besides, he's wealthy, eligible and reasonably attractive. I'm betting he's had enough women pursue him that he's been conned by outer packages before.''

''Maybe. But he still has hormones. Dump the sweatshirt, is my advice.''

Copper glints flashed in her eyes. ''The top three things he finds attractive in a woman are, quote—'Intelligence, a good sense of humor and compassion.'''

''Bunk. All ten bachelors said pretty much the same thing, give or take a few 'nice eyes' or 'friendly smile' here and there.'' Cameron flipped to the Target Market section of her plan, bypassed the demographic and geographic details and referred to the psychographic profile. ''Sanderson also says his idea of a perfect date is 'A picnic in the country miles from civilization.''' He snorted. ''Gimme a break.''

Two spots of pink stained her cheeks. ''I think that's lovely and romantic.''

''Of course you do. I'm not saying the dimwit

isn't smart, just that his idea of a perfect date might start with a picnic in the country, but it probably ends with a roll in the hay. Admitting that in print would be unprofessional and social suicide for any man. The nineties taught us political correctness.''

"I see."

He suddenly felt as if he'd kicked a puppy.

"Then your quote was a lie, too?"

Uh-oh. "Which quote?"

"You said your perfect date was 'Cuddling together on the couch, watching an old movie and being comfortable with long silences.' Was that just politically correct science fiction?"

The scenario he'd painted was alien, but oh-so appealing. Funny how he'd come full circle.

As a preschooler, he'd hated all the female attention that his ''adorable'' face induced. During elementary school, he'd thought all girls had cooties, but they'd slipped him love notes and Hershey's Kisses anyway. Then adolescence had hit, and what had once been a curse became a blessing. He couldn't say when the merciless pursuit of women had begun to pall.

Perhaps when he'd finally realized they didn't want him, so much as they did his reputation, though it was based more on assumption than fact.

Women expected him to entertain them, to charm them, to seduce them, and then to discard them. They wanted a dashing rake and high drama to remember in their old age, not a comfortable couch potato to watch old movies with the rest of their lives.

His perfect date quote had made his brothers laugh their asses off.

"I guess that answers my question," Lizzy said.

He snapped back to the present. "No, it wasn't science fiction, Lizzy. But I'd be lying if I said the cuddling and emotional closeness wouldn't make me want physical intimacy, too. I won't apologize for admitting a response any healthy heterosexual male would have—no matter how politically incorrect it sounds." His healthy heterosexual body was beginning to wake up to the conversation. And her eyes were filling with the feminine speculation he recognized so well. Jeez.

"Let's get back to your clothes for tomorrow," he suggested hastily. "It's supposed to be sunny and warmer. Wear something short and tight."

Amused horror replaced speculation. "And look like one of those pitiable women trying to turn back the clock and compete with coeds under twenty? Thanks, but no thanks."

"Who are you trying to kid?" The fact that she'd managed to fool him for years was irritating as hell. "I saw you earlier, Lizzy. You can compete."

Her lashes fluttered and dropped. She stared at her clasped hands.

His gaze wandered over her hair, freshly washed

and sweetly curling. Smelling of herbal shampoo, it looked impossibly soft....

Oh, God, he didn't *want* to wonder what those sable curls would feel like sifting through his fingers. What was *wrong* with him lately?

She looked up, and he felt the impact straight in his gut.

Her lips curved into the barest hint of a shy smile. "If I didn't know better, I'd think you actually complimented me on something unrelated to business."

An alarm sounded in his churning thoughts. "Anything that helps motivate Sanderson to ask you out is in my best business interest. Your legs are a product feature worth advertising," he said formally.

"Thank you," she said, equally formal.

Yet the alarm in his head trilled louder. "If you insist on wearing jeans, at least make sure they're tight. You'll need something brighter and tighter than that sweatshirt, too. Why don't you bring me a few options from your closet to choose from?"

She looked down at the logos covering the swell of her left breast, then unclasped her hands.

His throat tightened oddly.

Capable fingers he'd seen fly over a keyboard thousands of times lifted...lifted...then touched the puckered embroidery. Her finger pads skimmed the satiny threads in a hesitant caressing motion, producing sharp tugs of heat beneath the papers on his lap.

She raised doubtful eyes. ''I still think these logos will get his attention. It shows commitment to his cause—''

''Damn it, Lizzy, would you show some T and A and quit thinking so much! Jeez! If you can't find something sexy in your closet then go shopping with Susan. Or Rachel. Hell, Mrs. Doppler probably knows how to look sexy better than you do. Just stop arguing and let me do what you're blackmailing me to do, okay?''

With the animation of petrified wood, she nodded, rose and defied physics by covering the distance to her bedroom hallway without moving a muscle.

Cameron spent the next sixty seconds hoarsely uttering every foul curse in the Malloy brothers' extensive and colorful repertoire. It didn't help.

He still wanted to kiss her, despite deliberately crushing any similar desire on her part. He still wanted to tear her friggin' contract in half and call the whole deal off. He still knew that instead, he would hand Lizzy to Sanderson on a platter in order to protect his company's solvency. His fit of cursing had only changed one thing.

Now his throat hurt as much as his heart.

CHAPTER SEVEN

RACHEL SWITCHED OFF the Suburban's engine and twisted around to peer over the headrest. "Wait!" she warned her son as he reached for the door handle. "Let's review a few things so that we understand each other."

Beneath an Abercrombie & Fitch cap, dark blue eyes the exact color of her own rolled. But for once the expression in them was excitement, not resentment. "I *understand*. We've been over this a jillion times."

"So make it a jillion and one."

"Oh, Mom."

She cut her eyes to Elizabeth, who watched them from the passenger seat, clearly amused. "The last time I brought him to Zilker Park, he raced off before I could even get out of the car—"

"Mo-om—"

"After ten minutes of frantic searching, I found him at the opposite end of the park, playing Frisbee with a German shepherd bigger than he was."

"I was seven years old," he said, addressing

Elizabeth. "I'll never live it down. She reminds me every time I'm about to get out of the car."

Rachel caught her son's gaze. "Want me to switch to the Highland Mall story?"

Last year he'd lost track of time and failed to meet her at the food court as promised.

Ben's blush said he'd prefer the details of mall security's rescue mission to remain their little secret.

"Okay then," she said. "What are the rules?"

"I can't get anything that drools a lot," Ben recited in a singsong voice that didn't quite manage to sound bored. "I can't get anything that sheds a lot, runs a lot, barks a lot, chews a lot, pees a lot, poops a lot, or weighs over twenty-five pounds. I can't get my heart set on any dog until you've agreed it's a good match. *Now* can I go? Dad said he'd be at the cages waiting for us."

Her son was thirteen years old today and trying desperately to be cool about it—a feat both his audience and his impending birthday gift made almost impossible. His darting glances at Elizabeth were comical. And unsettling.

He wasn't a little boy anymore.

Rachel sighed. "Go on. But *no detours.* Go straight to your father."

He shoved the door open and paused. "You should go straight to Dad, too. Some jerk out there will think you're a 'hottie' and try to hit on you."

He flashed a silver grin at her gape, as if his embarrassed expression when she'd come out of the bedroom earlier hadn't almost made her turn around and change clothes.

His gaze slid to the younger woman. "Thanks again for the CD."

Elizabeth smiled warmly. "You're welcome. Happy birthday. Now go check out those cages and hope there's not a battery-operated stuffed animal in one of them, or your mom will make you adopt it."

He laughed, his braces bright against the flush from her attention. With a Joe Cool two-fingered salute, he tumbled out of the truck and slammed the door.

The fierce love swelling Rachel's heart also clogged her throat. The inconvenience of a smelly dog was nothing—*nothing*—against the happy, excited grin she hadn't seen in months.

God had surely sent Elizabeth to the Rosenfeld home last evening to set the stage for this precious moment.

Rachel had opened her door to the greeting, "Can you make me look sexy?" and been thankful her son was spending the night at a friend's. During the next four hours, she and Elizabeth exchanged true confessions, analyzed their respective situations, plotted Rachel's course of action, and made a quick trip to the mall.

Then they'd come home and finalized plans over a bottle of wine.

"He is *such* a cutie-pie," Elizabeth said now, staring pensively through the windshield.

The parked Suburban faced a vast expanse of withered grass swarming with ragtag touch football games, organized peewee soccer and a large milling crowd in the distance. Ben shuffle-strutted in ridiculously huge cargo pants toward the banner reading Pet Partners Placement Day.

Rachel cleared the emotion from her throat. "He is when he wants to be. That's the first time he's smiled at me since Steven left. Everything I do or say lately makes him mad, disgusted or embarrassed."

"Puberty," Elizabeth said simply.

It was much more complicated than that, but Rachel let it go. "Can you believe how tall he's gotten?"

"No! He's grown at least three inches since Memorial Day."

"Probably closer to four. Each day he changes a little more, pushes his boundaries a little harder. It's like living the toddler years all over again…except I can't wrestle him into adorable clothes anymore. *God*, I hate those pants."

As if on cue a breeze kicked up, turning Ben's lanky body into a human flagpole.

"Oh, Mom. Quit picking on his clothes. He's stylin'."

Rachel snorted. "He's a lemming. Has to wear *schmattes* like all the other kids."

"Shmatas?"

"Rags. Which wouldn't be so bad if they came from the thrift store. But no, they have to be *new* rags. I pay full price for clothes that look old and faded and three sizes too big. One good sneeze, and those stylin' pants will be stylin' socks."

Elizabeth laughed. "For what it's worth, I think you're smart to let Ben make personal choices you don't agree with—as long as his choices won't hurt him physically or psychologically. My mother allowed me to make my own decisions as a teenager, and it made me more mature."

It was on the tip of Rachel's tongue to suggest that Muriel Richmond had robbed her daughter of childhood, and was doing her best to ruin adulthood, too.

"Thanks," Rachel said instead. "I wish I could claim some deep maternal wisdom. But the truth is, without Steven to back me up, I've learned to save my energy for more important battles."

Her heartbeat accelerated. The task ahead slammed into her consciousness.

"Speaking of battles," Elizabeth said, adjusting the pink angora wool covering her from collarbone to just below her breasts. She tightened the dainty string bows behind her neck and back, and then—armor securely in place—met Rachel's eyes. "You ready to kick some butt?"

It had seemed like such a good idea last night. She'd hoped ignoring her misgivings all morning would make them disappear.

"Ra-a-chel. No guts, no glory, remember?"

"Yes. But I'm so nervous. Aren't you nervous? I'm so nervous." She lifted a hand palm down, her perfect French manicure trembling. "Look! I'm so nervous."

"We can do this."

"Speak for yourself."

"No, you'll speak for yourself. You're going to march up to Steven and tell him he's had his 'time and space to think,' that now it's time to be your husband. That you're tired of him avoiding you, and tired of Ben blaming you for a separation his father is at least equally responsible for causing.

"You're going to remind Steven that he left without giving you a clue he was unhappy, or a chance to work things out. You'll tell him y'all need to resolve your problems, not run away from them. You'll be understanding but firm, just like we practiced last night. Right?"

Rachel hesitated. "I've been giving that some thought…"

Angling her body, Elizabeth pulled her left knee onto the seat and braced her right platform sandal on the floor mat. "You're not wimping out on me, are you?"

In a just world, her pink-and-cream plaid short-shorts would've exposed a hint of cellulite.

"Rachel?"

She looked up guiltily. "Well, it *was* sort of my fault. I should've realized that Steven felt neglected—"

"Don't you dare feel guilty!"

Rachel winced. "I'm Jewish. Ask me not to breathe. I can *do* that. I don't think I can face Steven."

Frustration seethed in dark brown eyes. "If you insist on feeling guilty, then think about disappointing Ben. Don't let him fool you, he's as excited about seeing you and Steven together as he is about getting a dog. He'll be crushed if you don't make this a family event."

Rachel's shoulders slumped. "I know, I know."

"Then what are we waiting for? Chin up. Shoulders back. Let's go kick some butt."

Being a coward shouldn't be this hard. "No."

Concern joined frustration in Elizabeth's eyes. "I don't understand. You said you were going to take control of your destiny, just like me. We were going to walk side by side into battle. We were going to watch each other's backs. You were so fired up last night. What's happened since then to change your mind?"

"Sobriety."

Elizabeth blinked.

"Wine gives me false chutzpah," Rachel explained. She pressed three fingers against her chest and grimaced. "Orange juice only gives me heartburn."

"So that's your explanation? A joke?"

"It's no joke. You wouldn't happen to have a Tums handy, would you?"

With a disgusted growl, Elizabeth turned to reach for her door.

Rachel caught her friend's arm. "I'm sorry! I'm a yellow-bellied coward. But when I think about Steven seeing me dressed like this..." Oy! She could use some Pepto-Bismol, too.

"Is that what you're worried about? The way you're dressed?"

"I haven't worn anything this short, tight and uncomfortable in years. It's out of character. He'll be suspicious."

"He'll be surprised and pleased. Rachel, you look *fantastic*. Sultry and chic at the same time. You said yourself Steven thinks you look sexy in black."

Rachel's anxiety climbed. "It's been years since he said that. Years since I've *tried* to look sexy for him. Maybe I've been out of the loop too long. Maybe his tastes have changed. Maybe he's got his eye on some cute young thing—"

"Hey! You said he wasn't fooling around."

"He's not." She knew with unshakable certainty Steven would ask for a divorce before breaking his marital vows. "*But*...he can check out the merchandise for later, can't he?"

"Yes," Elizabeth conceded. "But you're the best-looking thing on the shelf. He'll reach for you."

"Maybe I'm not attractive to him anymore. Maybe I really look disgusting, not sultry and chic."

"Don't be ridiculous. You heard the saleslady. She said you're her first customer to do that body shirt justice.

"She works on commission."

Elizabeth rolled her eyes. "Okay, what about Ben? Do you trust your own son? He thinks you're a hottie."

"So now I have to worry about an Oedipus complex on top of everything else?"

"Get a grip, Rachel! You're grasping at straws to avoid confronting Steven. Trust me. You look beautiful."

Rachel rubbed sweaty palms on her skirt. "Don't get me wrong, I'm flattered. And hey, I think you look like every man's fantasy—a virgin slut. We can compliment each other all day, but it doesn't mean Steven and Cameron will think we're sexy. Maybe we just turn each other on."

"Rachel."

"You know what I mean."

Elizabeth started to say something, then closed her mouth. Her brow furrowed thoughtfully. "I see your point."

What? No denial? No rational argument? No marching-into-battle speech? To Rachel's horror, her friend's confident expression dissolved into obvious doubt.

"Oh, God, what time is it?" Elizabeth glanced at the dashboard clock and paled. "I'm supposed to meet Cameron near the hospitality tent in five minutes. There's no time to go home and change."

"Ben is probably wondering where I am," Rachel admitted sickly. "If I don't show up soon, he'll worry."

"Okay. Okay. Let's not overreact. We're stuck in an awkward situation, but we're confident, mature women. Attitude is everything, right? We can pull this off."

Speak for yourself.

"We're going to get out of this truck and walk up to Steven and Cameron with our heads held high. Now, on the count of three, we'll each open our doors. Ready?"

Or not.

"O-o-one," Elizabeth drawled, collecting her purse as Rachel did the same. "Two-o-o." They gripped their respective door handles, gazes locked. "Three!"

Neither woman moved.

Rachel stared into brown eyes that looked as irritated and panicked as she felt. The tension climbed. Oxygen grew thin. Was it better to die of suffocation or embarrassment?

"I'll give you a hundred bucks to change clothes with me," Elizabeth blurted.

Suddenly Rachel's embarrassing outfit seemed tame. "No!"

"One-fifty. And I'll let you keep the necklace."

"*No!*"

"Two hundred just for your body shirt. C'mon, Rachel, it only cost you fifty."

At full price. Oy! Her mother must be spinning in the grave.

Elizabeth's tone turned wheedling. "You could buy those earrings you showed me at Dillard's. They made your eyes look really really blue."

For an instant, the inner vision of bezel-set lapis distracted Rachel. She blinked back to sanity. "You'd say anything to get me undressed. I turn you on."

"Two twenty-five!" Elizabeth plucked a checkbook out of her purse. "It's highway robbery, but—"

"Stop!" Rachel glared at the plump perky swells

beneath pink angora wool. "There is not enough money in Saudi Arabia to make me wear your top."

Elizabeth glanced down, then over at the cleavage produced by underwire and elastic. "Why not? You'd look great in this top. Steven will step on his tongue if you wear this top."

"I'll step on my boobs if I wear that top."

"That's a little extreme, don't you think?"

"Look who's talking. You're ready to pay two hundred and twenty-five dollars for a shirt that'll be marked down to thirty-seven-fifty next week."

"Rachel, plee-ee-heez. I'm begging you."

"No."

"After that crack Cameron made about Mrs. Doppler, I *can't* meet him looking like this. If he felt sorry for me, I'd die. Die, do you understand?"

"Yes! I feel the same about Steven. Do you understand that I'm thirty-eight years old? I've had a baby. I've *breast-fed* a baby. Do you understand what that does to delicate tissue?"

"Angora is soft on delicate tissue."

"I can't wear that top."

"Pink is your color."

"I would if I could, but I can't."

"Black makes you look sallow."

Better sallow than saggy. "The answer's still no."

Elizabeth's eyes welled. "This is all your fault. You *made* me buy this top."

Rachel hardened her heart. "Because it looks great on you. Y-o-u. Not me. I need more material."

"You got that right. I've heard this spiel before."

"I need more coverage. I need more support." Rachel leaned over the console, gripped bare shoulders and gave them a shake. "For the love of God, woman, *I need a bra!*"

The sound of agitated breathing filled the Suburban's interior, along with the cloying smell of Obsession and Amarige Parfum on overwrought pulse points. *My fault, again,* Rachel thought. She'd made sure they both double-dabbed.

She blinked at Elizabeth and released her shoulders.

Elizabeth blinked back. Her mouth started to twitch.

Rachel snorted.

Elizabeth sputtered.

The dam cracked, and a torrent of tension, hysteria and dread gushed out. Just when one of them managed to plug up her giggles, the other would spring a leak, and off they went.

At last, a good three or four minutes later, only a few sporadic trickles remained.

Rachel wiped the moisture from beneath her eyes. Oy, her stomach muscles were sore. She hadn't laughed so hard since something had plopped in Steven's wineglass during a romantic terrace dinner at The Oasis on Lake Travis, and they'd looked up to find unexpected guests roosting in their oak tree canopy.

Shaking her head, she released a final chuckle, then drew a deep cleansing breath. It still smelled like the tester tray at a perfume counter, but she no longer felt sick with fear.

"Well, I'm glad we got that out of our systems," Elizabeth said, growing serious. "I fell off the wagon there a minute, but I'm back on now. I promised myself I was through hiding and playing it safe—and I am. I'm going out there, Rachel. With, or without you." She flipped down the windshield visor mirror, opened her purse and pulled out a compact and lipstick.

Rachel studied Elizabeth as she freshened her makeup. In the past, her unrelenting professionalism, role as office mediator and stodgy wardrobe had redirected attention from herself to others. But ever since she'd quit her job, she'd grown more confident, more...self-aware, in a way that had nothing to do with vanity. It was as if her true spirit had been liberated from inside the woman they'd all "known." She almost seemed to glow from within.

This woman looked vibrant and alive, not quiet and controlled. As fascinating to know as she was fascinated with others. This woman was truly beautiful, not merely pretty.

And she wasn't letting the man she loved slip out of her life without a fight.

Elizabeth capped her lipstick and turned. "Are you in, or out?"

In answer, Rachel jerked open her door, slid from behind the wheel to the parking lot, and tugged her black stretch denim skirt back down to three inches above the knee.

She centered her silver belt buckle inlaid with turquoise. Adjusted the low square neckline of her black body shirt. Positioned her turquoise pendant, a fifth-year anniversary gift from Steven, to nestle just so. Settled the chain link strap of her dainty good-for-nothing-but-holding-lipstick purse over her shoulder and then, as ready as she'd ever be, locked and slammed her door.

Her heart was racing like a young girl's.

She hadn't spent time with her husband in over three months, though she did speak to him on the phone occasionally. Brief, stilted conversations. About Ben's slipping grades, Ben's increasing hostility, Ben's Bar Mitzvah, now only two weeks away. Steven always honked in the driveway for their son, and never came inside the house afterward.

Allowing Ben to adopt the dog she'd always vetoed in the past had guaranteed that Steven couldn't avoid her today.

Just then, a Jeep filled with boisterous young men

wearing ATO frat shirts approached, the driver obviously seeking a parking space. Wolf whistles erupted, along with invitations to join their party as the Jeep rolled past. Laughing, Rachel was glad her friend's short-shorts and Angora top were an unqualified success.

A door slammed. She turned and realized Elizabeth had only this moment gotten out of the truck.

Rachel's head whipped back toward the Jeep. One muscular hottie met her eyes, clutched his heart and yelled, "I'm in love."

Oy!

In a daze, she walked slowly to the front of the Suburban. Amazing what a little flirting from a man half one's age could do for one's ego. A man's ego needed periodic boosts, too. Dressing this way for Steven could only make him feel good.

Rachel joined her waiting friend.

"Well? Do you trust *them?*" Elizabeth asked, smirking.

"We can really do this, can't we?"

"That's the spirit! Chin up. Shoulders back. Lookin' good, Mom. Dad'll step on his tongue." Elizabeth's gaze hardened. "Now, are you ready to talk some sense into him?"

Rachel fluffed her hair and narrowed her eyes. "Let's go kick some butt."

CHAPTER EIGHT

HE WAS CUTER THAN his dimwit picture.

His cheeks were slightly round, his nose a bit pug. Both were smattered with freckles, and a dimple centered his square chin. He wore a blue baseball cap turned backward. His sandy brown hair tufted through the hole above the closure tabs. A navy polo-style shirt displayed an S-mart Computers logo where the famous horse icon would normally gallop.

Larry Sanderson looked more like Opie Taylor of Mayberry than a brilliant corporate leader, Elizabeth decided. It was hard to believe he owned and operated the national company that had manufactured the laptop computer facing both him and two female volunteers.

The three were set up at separate tables in a wide grassy corridor formed by double-stacked portable kennels. Dogs on one side, cats on the other. A diverse crowd flowed past both rows. Excited barks, an occasional distressed meow, and human chatter competed with piped music from a classic rock station doing a live remote.

The smell of spun sugar, popcorn and French fries added to the carnival-like atmosphere. The volunteers had their hands full keeping unattended kids from feeding the animals.

Leaning against two cat kennels, Elizabeth watched a barrio gang member and redneck cowboy bump shoulders to peer inside a cage. All she could make out was a pink tongue darting through wire, but they must've seen something incredibly cute, because they looked at each other and grinned.

The next time a riot broke out in this country, she mused, the government should send in litters of puppies instead of the National Guard. Hate couldn't survive an onslaught of ecstatic licks and thumping tails.

She straightened from the kennels and glanced inside. The adult tabby and Siamese ignored her, as remote as Sphinxes, which was exactly why she'd chosen to loiter on this side of the tracks.

She had a big backyard and a true love of dogs, but very little time to spend with a pet. Separating herself from soulful please-take-me-home eyes was her wisest, and kindest, strategy.

Her gaze moved to Ben and Rachel, who were still talking with one of the women volunteers. No heart-to-heart with Steven had happened yet. It had taken this long for Rachel to agree on Ben's choice of dog.

Cameron had shown up late, hot and sweaty from

another ball-throwing session with Miguel. Apparently the teen wasn't extending his arm properly, and Cameron felt honor-bound to correct the problem. Upon arrival, he'd ducked inside KVUE's hospitality tent to grab a "quick" Coke. He'd asked her to wait until he got back before making a move, but he was taking forever.

Meanwhile, Larry's line had dwindled to one last applicant. Now he and a grandmotherly woman rose from their chairs simultaneously. He took her hand in both of his and gave it a pat. She walked away smiling.

He was alone!

She'd waited an hour for this chance for a little privacy. No telling how long it would last. She had to grab the opportunity.

Stomach fluttering, Elizabeth left the sheltering kennels and headed for Larry's table. He saw her coming and remained standing, his greenish-brown eyes lighting with wary interest as she approached.

Wariness was good. It supported her theory that he'd been pursued by enough aggressive women to suspect a wolf in virgin slut's clothing.

She walked the last few steps, hoping the paper she clutched wasn't marked with sweat prints. "Hi. Can you take my adoption application?"

"Absolutely." Smiling, he indicated the opposite folding chair. "Have a seat and we'll get you started."

Relax, she ordered herself as they both got settled. *If he says no, at least you'll still be able to live with yourself.*

She nodded toward the stack of applications by his computer. "Looks like the day is a big success. Congratulations."

He swept a pleased look over the organized chaos. "Thanks. Between KVUE's advance promotion and this beautiful weather, we've had a great turnout. About sixty percent of the animals we brought today have already been placed."

Frowning, she looked at Ben. Oh, she hoped he wasn't too late! The time it had taken him to get Rachel's consent might've cost him the dog he'd fallen in love with.

"I'm sorry. If you preselected a pet from our kennel cages, you might be disappointed," Larry said, obviously mistaking her distress. "But there are still quite a few animals back at the shelter that need a good home. We'll find you a good match. Let me take a look at your application."

She passed him her completed form.

Watching him scan her personal data, she saw his gaze flicker and stop, then move on. He either made the connection between her occupation and his fellow eligible bachelor, or he was surprised a vice president of any company would dress for a red-light district.

"Well, I see that you own a house with a fenced

backyard. That's good. And you're looking for quiet companionship, not protection, so maybe a cat? Oops. I see you're not a cat person. You prefer dogs. 'Real' dogs, not any breed that has the word 'toy' in front of it, or yips instead of barks.'' A smile tugged at his mouth as he looked up. ''Most of the larger dogs Pet Partners received were left in backyards with no playtime stimulation or additional exercise. Naturally, they dug in flower beds and chewed lawn furniture and went wild with joy when their owners *did* step outside to throw them some food.''

Elizabeth's heart squeezed at the picture he painted. ''I'm a jogger. I could take a dog on a leash with me, if he was young and healthy and wouldn't bark at neighbors.''

''He? Does that mean you want a male?''

''No. Either sex would be fine,'' she heard herself say.

''Excellent! Let me enter some of this data in our match program.''

She watched him type busily and couldn't seem to open her mouth and tell him she had no intention of adopting an animal.

He focused once more on her application. ''You have no other pets. That's good. They might feel jealous over your divided attention. Destructive behavior often results.'' His rising gaze lingered on pink angora before meeting her eyes with Opie in-nocence. "What about a boyfriend?"

"A boyfriend?"

"You know, one of those belligerent creatures who growl and snap when another man invades his territory. Do you have one of those hanging around the house?"

Elizabeth smiled. "Is that really relevant?"

"Just being thorough."

Hormonal flirting, she thought. His brain clearly wasn't involved. "Well, the answer is no. I'm way too old to want a boyfriend."

His grunt was skeptical. "Not from where I sit—" he checked the top of her application "—Elizabeth."

"Then you obviously need to look at the situation from my perspective—" she held his gaze "—*Larry.*"

Hazel eyes sharpened. Suddenly she had no trouble at all imagining him presiding in a boardroom, making astute executive decisions.

"Have we met before?" he asked.

"No. I read the 'most eligible bachelor' article in the newspaper. You're Larry Sanderson, right?"

"That's right." His expression hardened and cooled. "Apparently every unmarried woman in Austin read that article. I wish to God I hadn't agreed to be featured." He paused. "Please tell me

you're here because you want my help matching
you with a suitable dog.''

"I wish I could," she said fervently, "but de-
ceiving one person at a time is all I can stomach.
I'm here because I want your help matching me
with a suitable man—whom I've already preselected, by the way." *No guts, no glory.* "Would
you go out on four dates with me?"

He studied her with both amazement and distaste.
"You're more creative than the others, I'll give you
that. But I'm not interested. I prefer to do the asking, thank you."

She offered an apologetic smile. "I've given you
the wrong impression. I don't normally dress like
this. And I'm not interested in you romantically,
though I do know a lot about you, and any woman
who *did* become romantically involved with you
would be very lucky." Lord, she was making a
mess of this. "I thought dating with no pressure
might sound good to you right about now."

"No pressure?"

"Yes. That eligible bachelor article was like yelling "Gold!" to women mining for wealthy hus-
bands. You've probably got picks swinging at you
from all directions." She took heart from the startled amusement in his eyes. "Dating me could give
you a restful break until the gold fever dies down.
You wouldn't have to be charming or funny or even
polite. You wouldn't have to constantly measure

your date's sincerity. You wouldn't have to worry about whether or not she likes you, or only your material success. I don't want anything from you. Nothing, that is, except your escort on four friendly dates.''

He cocked his head, looking intrigued in spite of himself. ''I probably shouldn't ask, but…why?''

''Because it's my last chance to open the eyes of the man I love.'' Elizabeth paused, her skin prickling, and traced the source unerringly to a tall man standing outside the KVUE tent in the distance.

Her heart lurched.

''If you want my help, Elizabeth, you'll have to be more specific than that. How about telling me the full story?''

She jerked her gaze back to alert hazel eyes. ''I'll have to give you the condensed version. The full story covers fifteen years.''

CAMERON ENTERED the bright sunlight and pulled up short, a limp cup of iced Coke in hand. He needed to get farther away, or risk getting sucked back in. But after spending the past twenty minutes in the dimly lit hospitality tent, he couldn't see a damn thing.

Man, he thought he'd *never* get out of there!

KVUE's promotion director had corralled him to discuss a trade with one of his clients, Southwest Toyota. The station wanted a Celica GT to offer as a hole-in-one prize during its annual charity golf tournament.

Not a bad deal, actually. For the cost of insuring the car against loss, his client would get thousands of dollars' worth of free airtime. If some lucky bastard accidentally *did* make the shot…that was even better. The dealership would collect insurance and count it as a sale.

He took a sip of watery Coke, walked toward the end of a long row of cat kennels on his right—and stopped again.

No dark-haired woman loitered in the shadows looking ready to call out, "Hey sailor, wanna good time?"

His gaze shot to the dimwit's table about forty yards ahead.

Lizzy sat talking to the man he was beginning to dislike more intensely with each passing day. Never mind that their paths had never crossed. Or that Larry Sanderson had no inkling of Lizzy's plan. He'd still managed to screw up Cameron's life big time.

As if sensing his glare, Lizzy stopped talking and looked straight at him.

Pre-dimwit days, his pulse would've stayed steady.

She refocused quickly on her "target" and continued speaking, her manner earnest and intense. Though Cameron could only see Sanderson from the back, his body language spoke of riveted attention.

And why not? Her adoption application revealed she was a successful businesswoman. Her articulate speech would tell him she was intelligent, educated and interesting. Her provocative clothes advertised she was an uninhibited "single hot babe." And her curvy body screamed "Satisfaction guaranteed!"

The guy was probably thanking God for the miracle manifested before him.

And Cameron had dressed the miracle as surely as if he'd tied those one-tug-and-they're-history bows behind her neck and back. His taunt the day before had backfired. She'd turned hurt into anger and gotten revenge. He narrowed his eyes. She knew damn well he hadn't meant for her to look *this* sexy!

No doubt about it. Unless Larry was blind, gay or already in love with another woman, he'd ask Lizzy out.

The cup Cameron squeezed collapsed.

He hopped back, hand outstretched, crushed ice and soda gushing out. As his wrist and forearm dripped, he looked down at the spatters of wet denim decorating his left leg. Jeez.

"Let me take that," a masculine voice offered.

The soggy cup was removed from Cameron's fingers, then replaced with a stack of rumpled paper napkins stained with something brown. He looked up to see Steven Rosenfeld, a carton of chili fries in one hand and a cup in the other, walking toward a trash bin close to the tent. He tossed in the cup, popped a fry into his mouth and headed back.

Earlier, Cameron had come upon Ben crouched beside a kennel, pleading with his parents to adopt the large black dog inside. The timing had been wrong for more than brief hellos, Cameron had decided.

But he'd been bug-eyed suspicious about Rachel's tight black clothes and visible cleavage.

Blotting his forearm, he waited for her husband to draw near. "Thanks. That was good timing."

"Thank my stomach. Want a bite?"

Cameron shook his head.

Shrugging, Steven stuffed three chili fries into his mouth at once.

Hiding his surprise, Cameron noted how different he seemed from the laughing man swaying in a conga line at The Banana Tree Restaurant last December. His dark silver-threaded hair was untrimmed, his blue oxford shirt unironed, his khaki slacks too snug at the waist. He'd never been as warm and gregarious as his wife, but he'd always exuded a quiet strength and intelligence that was equally attractive. Susan had once called him a "deep hunk."

Today there was an edgy, strained air about him

that Cameron recognized all too well. Cumulative stress did that to a man.

Eyeing Steven nervously, Cameron peeled off a layer of damp paper and handed it over before continuing to mop his frozen skin. "You've got chili on your mouth."

Grunting, Steven scrubbed his lips. "Be glad I'm a slob, or I wouldn't have had extra napkins."

Good point. "I'm surprised Rachel's even letting you eat that crap."

"I pretty much live on fast food these days."

"Yeah? She's a health cop at the office—" Cameron wiped his last finger "—and has the nose of a bloodhound. I can't even sneak stuff past her under my coat." Wadding the soaked napkins into a ball, he spun around and aimed at a nearby trash bin. "What's your secret?"

"Rachel and I have been separated about three months, now. I thought you knew."

Cameron's shot fell five feet wide of the mark.

He turned around slowly. Shock held him mute. Steven and Rachel, *separated?*

They were one of the lucky couples. Good for each other as well as in love. She kept him from becoming too aloof; he kept her from crossing the line into theatrics. Married fifteen years and still going strong—or so he'd thought. What had happened?

Cameron finally pulled himself together. "I'm sorry, man. I didn't know."

"I can see that. Guess she took it in stride, if she went about business as usual and didn't tell you." Bitterness tinged Steven's voice.

"Wait a minute. Don't jump to conclusions based on me. Hell, I'm so busy all day stepping over bullshit, a horn could hook me in the butt and I wouldn't notice! One thing I *do* know is that Rachel loves you." Cameron's chest tightened. "She must really be hurting."

He followed Steven's turbulent gaze to the center table in the grassy corridor.

Rachel sat with her arm around Ben, nodding at the volunteer who appeared to be going over points on an instruction sheet. Apparently the Rosenfelds had qualified to adopt their dog of choice. The boy suddenly laughed and looked up at his mother.

Even from here, Cameron could see the love glowing in her expression.

"Yeah, she looks real torn up," Steven said in a flat tone. "It's a terrible thing, Cameron, for a father to be jealous of his own son."

Whoa!

"Oh, God, no," Steven said, reading Cameron's incredulous thoughts. "There's nothing unnatural going on between Rachel and Ben. She's a wonderful mother. He's a normal boy with lots of interests—including girls. The problem is *me*."

"I'm sure you're exaggerating," Cameron protested lamely. His mind scrambled for an excuse to leave.

"No. Deep down some part of me has always resented Ben. I want to come first with Rachel. And I can't handle knowing that I don't." He lifted his free hand, shoved thick hair back from his forehead and clutched a fistful of strands. "Is that sick, or what?"

Cameron didn't know and didn't want to. Maybe he could say he'd left something behind in the hospitality tent.

Steven released his hair. The disheveled result matched the drowning-man panic in his eyes, and words poured from his throat, drenched in guilt. "I'd hoped it would get better as he grew older and more independent. But when I started the new job, I was determined to make myself indispensable. So I worked late most nights, and went to the office two out of four weekends a month, and Rachel took up the slack at home. She got even more involved in Ben's activities, not less."

Cameron looked to Lizzy for help. Nope. Still immersed in conversation.

"The free time I did have," Steven continued, "Rachel insisted we spend as a family. Being Ben's parents was more important to her than being a husband and wife to each other."

One word about their sex life and I'm outta here, Cameron thought.

"I love my son. That's the hell of it. The resentment was tearing me apart…and he's a smart kid. He would've figured out how I felt pretty soon, and probably blamed himself. I couldn't let that happen. And I couldn't—" Steven stopped and swallowed hard, his struggle for control painful to witness. "I couldn't tell Rachel why I left. I don't know why I'm telling you."

Despairing dark eyes locked onto Cameron as if he were the last lifeboat on the Titanic. The happy crowd, cold in its oblivion, swirled around the drama going down in its midst.

But his boat was full, damn it! He didn't have room for another burden.

As his silence stretched, the sound of a nearby toddler wailing for cotton candy seemed amplified.

"Forget it," Steven blurted. "It's not your problem. God, I'm sorry. I don't know what I was thinking." His bleak gaze returned to Rachel and Ben; his forgotten carton of fries tipped dangerously toward the ground.

Jeez. Cameron wished like hell fate hadn't spilled his Coke the exact moment Rachel's husband was ready to spill his guts.

He moved closer, squeezed Steven's shoulder and gently turned him around. "C'mon, buddy. Let's find a quieter place to talk."

After guiding Steven to the trash bin, Cameron deposited the fries, then steered the unprotesting man to the spot Lizzy had occupied earlier. Fewer people walked all the way to this end of the cat kennels, and the ones who did were usually headed for parked cars.

With only a large scruffy tomcat and an elegant Siamese as their audience, Cameron felt a little less conspicuous and freer to speak his mind. "First off, have you talked to anyone besides me about how you feel?"

Steven shook his head. "I thought time away from Rachel would give me a chance to get my act together. And being alone with Ben has worked out great. We're a lot closer. But…even talking on the phone with Rachel brings back ugly feelings. Every conversation is 'Ben this,' and 'Ben that.'" He made a disgusted sound. "I told you, I'm abnormal."

For sure he was tormented, and needed help. "You think you're the first father ever to feel like you do? No way. You've got to stop beating yourself up and learn to deal with it. You love Ben. You love Rachel. An experienced professional can help you sort out the 'ugly' stuff and throw it away. But I'm not telling you anything you don't already know. Why haven't you talked to a counselor?"

Mutinous pride and resistance crept into Steven's expression, and answered the question. Maybe in

L.A. or New York men went to a therapist more often than a dentist. But in Austin, a man often kept his problems to himself far too long before admitting he couldn't solve them alone.

Cameron sighed, thinking how many compliments he got in his great smile.

"Don't be stupid," he said bluntly. "You gave it a shot by yourself and now the whole family's suffering, not just you. Forget pride and see a counselor. You and Rachel should both go."

"But it's *my* problem."

"No. How you act affects her, and vice versa. She's just as responsible. I watched my brother and sister-in-law screw up what they had by refusing to share feelings with each other. They spent the next nine years alone before they came to their senses and 'fessed up.'"

Steven moved to the front of the stacked kennels, braced a hand on the top corner and peered inside. "I think Rachel's relieved that I'm gone. In two months, she's never once asked me to come back. She's never even tried to find out *why* I left."

The Siamese cat emitted a gravelly yowl, walked forward and pressed one side of her chocolate face against the kennel door. Steven poked two fingers through the wire and scratched behind her ear, his posture defeated.

Cameron's impatience flared. "Maybe she's never

asked you why because she's afraid of the answer. Did you think of that?''

Steven stiffened.

''She still loves you, idiot! The last thing she wants to hear is that you don't love her anymore. If she doesn't ask, she can pretend everything will be okay. Just like you're pretending. But what you're both doing is wasting time that you can't ever get back.''

Withdrawing his fingers from the kennel, Steven turned around. Beneath the doubt and dejection in his eyes, a tiny flame of annoyance burned.

Heartened, Cameron pushed on. ''I guarantee you she's blaming herself, or imagining all sorts of reasons worse than the truth for why you left. Talk to her. Today. Tell her what she *wants* to hear first—that you love and miss her—and she'll accept the rest. Then you can work on your problems together as a team.''

''You really think she's blaming herself?''

''There's only one sure way to find out. Will you just talk to her, for God's sake?''

Steven's gaze moved suddenly to the left and lit with gladness, hunger and tentative hope. He drew himself up straight.

Knowing what he'd see, Cameron turned around. Rachel walked toward them. An alternate-universe Rachel in a black ensemble that turned male heads, though she had eyes only for Steven.

"One last thing, buddy," Cameron added softly. "She didn't dress like a parent to meet you here today. She dressed like a wife who wants you back home...including in her bed."

At Steven's startled glance, Cameron winked, then turned and headed for a stand of oak trees edging the soccer fields.

CHAPTER NINE

TEN MINUTES LATER, stretched out on a picnic table with hands clasped behind his head, Cameron stared up at a jigsaw puzzle of gnarled branches, rusty oak leaves and deep blue sky.

After advising Steven and Rachel to quit pretending and admit their relationship problems, Cameron could no longer ignore his own. The statement that had plagued him since last Monday sprang uncaged from his guilty conscience.

I figured if you ever got interested in my personal life, you'd at least ask questions once in a while.

Lizzy had figured, huh? That was more than he'd allowed himself to do in ten years. Why hadn't he shown more interest in her personal life?

The answer hit him with the force of a truth long suppressed.

He hadn't shown more interest because he'd known—he'd always known—she felt more for him than any colleague, friend or employee should.

Not that she'd ever acted any way but friendly, professional and as bluntly honest as a sister. She hadn't. But he'd picked up signals. Oh, yeah, he'd known she had romantic feelings for him, and was as emotionally tethered to him as to her job.

So he hadn't praised or thanked her nearly enough. He hadn't asked questions about her private life. He hadn't socialized with her outside of the office. He hadn't learned that she wanted a large family, or that she needed to trim the cedar bush next to her garage.

Because if he had crossed the line into her personal space…she might've been encouraged to reveal emotions he'd be forced to tell her he didn't share. Their professional relationship might've been damaged. Worst-case scenario, she might've quit her job.

God forbid he should let her move on to greater happiness if it meant Malloy Marketing would lose a top-notch talent!

Lowering his gaze, he studied his crossed sneakers morosely.

Despite his selfishness—actually, because of his selfishness—she would move on to greater happiness soon. If not with Sanderson, then with the next man she "targeted" for a husband. Cameron had lost the power to keep her tethered close.

His strategy of sustained disinterest had finally killed her romantic interest in him. And, in one of life's twisted ironies, he'd finally begun feeling more for her than any colleague, friend or employer should. The adage What Goes Around, Comes Around had never seemed so apt.

Now she held the position of power.

Cameron narrowed his eyes, one sneaker twitching. If anyone had told him last Sunday he'd spend this one tied up in knots over Lizzy, he would have laughed. Now he couldn't stop wondering what would've happened if he'd responded to her subtle signals years ago, instead of being a first-class prick.

He had a horrible feeling that he'd missed out on something wonderful, but for the life of him, he couldn't decide which was worse.

Knowing he only had himself to blame for losing her affection.

Or knowing he could probably win it back...if he only dared to try.

STANDING AT THE TOP of the grassy knoll in front of the Austin American Statesman building, Rachel searched the crowded slope facing Town Lake and the Congress Avenue bridge. Families, couples and tourists dotted the prime viewing area, awaiting sunset and one of Austin's most unique sights. From mid-March to late October, the warm humid space between the bridge's expansion joints was home to the largest urban bat colony in the world. Over one and a half million Mexican free-tailed bats would emerge from under the bridge at dusk to feed on as much as thirty thousand pounds of insects, according to Ben. Rachel suppressed a shudder.

She could have happily gone the rest of her life without seeing the exodus, but Ben was milking his birthday wish list to the max. He'd done a science report last year on the bats, yet had never seen them, and felt gypped.

Since the unseasonably warm fall had delayed the colony's migration, he'd requested to end his full day here…so here she'd agreed to come.

But where the devil were he and his dad?

The football blanket Steven had removed earlier from the trunk of his car had been green. Hard to spot on the groomed turf…

Ah, there it was! She frowned in annoyance.

Served her right for lagging behind while they staked a claim on the grass. The only available space they'd left her on the blanket was next to the eighty-five-pound drooling, shedding, running, barking, chewing, peeing, pooping creature she'd agreed to let Ben adopt.

The three-year-old Labrador-Rottweiler mixed breed had belonged to a twelve-year-old boy who'd moved overseas with his parents. Which possibly explained the animal's immediate joyful response to Ben, but not her son's reciprocal love at first sight. Her resistance had proved no match against their uncanny instant bond.

Heading down the slope, she thought wistfully that there would have been plenty of room on the blanket if he'd fallen for the adorable dachshund she'd lobbied to adopt.

She drew close and Ben sat up, pulling the leashed dog into a sitting position, also.

He looped an arm around glossy black fur and grinned. "Hi, Mom! We saved you a spot by us, didn't we, Sport?"

At the sound of his name, Sport lavished his new owner's face with adoring licks so enthusiastic he knocked off Ben's cap and had him sputtering and yelping with laughter.

She started to object, then closed her mouth. What were a few germs compared to that happy sound?

Looking past the boy and dog, she met Steven's gaze. He lay on his side, elbow propped, head in hand, his expression intense, as it had been during their private talk at the park. A thousand shared emotional and physical intimacies reflected in his eyes, making her heart ache and beat faster at the same time.

She loved him so much. She'd missed him so much. She'd cheated them both so much by allowing motherhood to become her defining role.

Despite his guilt-ridden confession of jealousy, she'd never known a more patient or loving father than Steven. She was the one at fault, for giving him cause to doubt his importance in her life.

No more! Rachel promised herself. They'd started a dialogue they should have begun years ago. She had no intention of letting him shut the doors of communication—or any other door that kept them apart—ever again.

Lowering her knees to the blanket, she admitted they had much to discuss and resolve in the coming weeks. Some of their issues might require professional assistance. But the problem she found most distressing, their mutual loss of confidence in their desirability to the other, required only privacy to correct.

She was encouraged to catch Steven eyeing her legs as she struggled to sit in the short tight skirt.

And what do you expect when you dress like a kurveh?

Rachel heard the exasperated voice as clearly as if her mother were standing a foot away.

While Ben patted the blanket and commanded the dog to lie down, she stretched her legs out straight in front of her and held them firmly together. If anyone farther down the slope actually made the effort to look up her skirt, they'd have to get their jollies elsewhere. And Mama would have to get in someone else's head.

Sighing, she picked up Ben's fallen cap, a duplicate of two she'd replaced in the past three months, then reached over Sport and plopped it on her son's head. "You lose this one and you're paying us back. No more gravy train. Understood?"

Ben cast her an aggrieved look from under the cap's bill. "You already told me a zillion times."

She waited until he squirmed before saying sweetly, "The correct answer is, 'Yes, oh wise and generous parents who are teaching me to be a responsible person instead of a spoiled brat. I understand.'"

He turned to his father, whose expression was uncompromising.

Ben sighed. "Yes, oh wise and generous parents who are teaching me not to be a spoiled brat. I understand."

Close enough. She didn't miss his covert glance from one parent to the other, or the fact that he seemed more content than upset by their united front.

As the dog panted happily beneath Ben's stroking fingers, she talked with Steven about his parents' plans for the Bar Mitzvah weekend. They were flying in from Dallas with a group of about twelve Rosenfeld relatives on Friday morning. Had they decided to stay at the hotel with everyone else, or at the house?

"They're staying at the hotel," Steven told her. "Mother says we'll have enough to worry about without the added stress of company."

Oh-oh. "Sounds like she's just being polite. You know they'd love to have more time with Ben. Unless she wants the chance to feel a little pampered at a hotel, they should stay with us. I'll call her tonight." Rachel's heartbeat increased. "You can talk to her, too, and between us, we should be able to convince her it's no imposition. All right?"

Behind Ben's back, she held her husband's sharpened gaze. She'd all but handed him an engraved invitation to come home and stay the night.

"All right," he agreed in a tone that made her stomach jump.

An excited buzz broke out among the relaxed crowd.

"Mom! Dad!" Ben twisted around, capturing their attention. "They're starting to come out—" he whipped back to face the water "—look!"

Rachel followed his pointing finger to the Congress Avenue bridge. The reinforced concrete structure spanned approximately three hundred yards of Town Lake on the Colorado River. Respectable skyscrapers formed a cosmopolitan backdrop, at odds with the Roman aqueduct style of the bridge.

The archways and support columns beneath were interesting, but hardly unique. At least, that's what she'd always thought.

But as the first column of bats rose like a wisp of smoke against the violet sky, her perception began to change. From this distance, they looked like small individual birds—not the rabid, blood-sucking, soul-stealing, disease-ridden vermin Ben had assured her was a bum rap perpetuated by ignorance and horror flicks.

A second, thicker column streamed out and up, lifting the tiny hairs on Rachel's arms. The third, fourth and fifth belched forth from the underbelly so densely packed she wondered how they avoided collision, even with their sophisticated sonar systems. The sky became a living canvas of swirling black on deepening blue, a truly awesome spectacle.

Unconsciously, she scooted closer to the Sherman tank covered in soft fur. Reaching behind her son's shoulders, she found her husband's warm hand waiting to enfold hers in a near bruising grip, as if he'd never let her go. Ben leaned back slightly against the support of their linked arms. Sport turned his head and laid his drooling muzzle across her knees. Her eyes welled. There were no adequate words to express her emotions.

When Sport's tail thump-thump-thumped his joy against the blanket, Rachel lifted her free hand…hesitated…then slowly patted his head.

She couldn't have said it any better.

GRUNT-SNIP! Grunt-snip! Grunt-snip!

Cameron wielded the hedge clippers with such vicious force the aluminum ladder he stood on rattled and swayed. The thing was rusty and unsafe, but his best option for reaching the top of the eight-foot cedar bush next to Lizzy's garage.

Two days ago he'd added Steven and Rachel to a full boat of worries. Something had to get tossed overboard. This bush had weighed heavy on Cameron's mind ever since he'd clapped eyes on the thing. This evening, his Jaguar had sort of steered itself here instead of toward home after leaving the office parking garage. Big mistake.

Lizzy had answered the door, flustered and excited, explaining that Sanderson had just phoned. Pet Partners had received a golden retriever that would be perfect for her to adopt. He would cut through red tape and deliver "Lucy" personally tonight, if Lizzy wanted.

She'd not only wanted, she'd invited him to stay for dinner—if he wanted.

He'd wanted.

Duh, Cameron had thought.

"That's great," he'd lied. "I'll be finished and gone by then. Give me some tools, go about your business and pretend I'm not here."

And damned if she hadn't taken him at his word and done just that, disappearing inside to get ready for her second date.

Grunt-snip! Grunt-snip! Grunt-snip!

What would she wear this time? A bikini? Hell, by the third date she'd probably go buck naked!

He'd have to warn her about appearing overeager, too easily won. That was his job, after all. To keep her from scaring off Sanderson before his friggin' paws had been all over her at least four different friggin' times!

Cameron blew out a breath through his teeth. This venomous rage was a new experience. Horrible and horrifying, like snakes twisting in his belly. Being jealous poisoned his view of everything and everyone around him.

He didn't like it. He didn't want it. He didn't have time for it. And he didn't have the faintest clue how to deal with it.

For the time being, he settled for pretending every pungent branch he lopped off was Sanderson's head.

The man wasn't blind, gay or in love with another woman, and he'd lost no time asking Lizzy for a date. On Sunday, after his volunteer shift at Zilker Park they'd gone straight to Chuy's Restaurant on Barton Springs Road. Cameron had tailed them to the parking lot and been startled, then downright pissed.

Chuy's was *his* favorite restaurant. Had been since before Tex-Mex food and tacky decor was chic. Still was, for that matter, even though nowadays his dates preferred snotty maître d's and extensive wine lists over sneering velvet Elvis paintings and five choices of salsa. Their loss, not his.

He simply ate his Chuychanga burritos alone, and enjoyed not having to exert effort beyond chewing or mustering a beer burp.

Cameron paused, the sting of sweat in his eyes nothing compared with the red-hazed burn of watching Lizzy being escorted, paw on her lower back, inside the restaurant.

Grunt-snip! Grunt-snip! Grunt-snip!

He'd fidgeted and fumed for five minutes in his car, said the hell with it—and decided to spy. Inside the Mil Pescados Bar, she'd seemed charmed by the fanciful painted fish hanging from the ceiling. Almost as enthralled as Sanderson had appeared with her.

The sight of that same big paw roaming Lizzy's bare arms and back had curled Cameron's hands into white-knuckled fists. He'd had to leave the restaurant before he gave in to his need to rearrange a few freckles, and maybe a few ribs.

Grunt-snip! Grunt-snip!

Cameron whacked off the last reachable protruding branch, paused to catch his breath and undo three of his shirt buttons, then stepped down two rungs on the ladder and attacked the bush again.

Through the sound of slashing blades and his own grunts, he heard Lizzy's front door open and close. Without looking, he was aware of every step she took while approaching the ladder.

"O-oh, my God. What are you *doing?*" she wailed.

Jeez. "What do you think—" *Grunt-snip!* "—I'm doing?"

"I don't know. It *looks* like you're making a bonsai tree out of my cedar bush! Would you *stop* a minute?"

He took his sweet time. First wiping his forehead on the shoulder seam of his wilted dress shirt, then shifting on the creaking ladder, then propping an elbow on the nearest rung, and then—cautioning himself to remain indifferent even if she wore a bikini—finally looking down.

She was swaddled from neck to polished pink toenails in a bulky blue terry-cloth robe. Clutching the lapels primly together with one hand, she supported a white towel turban with the other. Her heart-shaped face was scrubbed free of makeup, and lit by the setting sun at his back. She looked mad enough to knock his ass off the ladder.

And he wanted to make love to her every way he knew how.

Plus one he didn't, but wanted to try.

Son of a bitch!

She glared from him to the results of his labor. "You said you were going to *trim* it, not mutilate it."

"Don't worry. I'll clean up the shape nice and pretty for Larry before I leave."

"Larry?" She wrinkled her nose. "What's he got to do with it? All I care about is hiding the ugly drainpipe behind my bush. If you cut off any more from the top, that won't be possible."

"Yeah, and it won't be possible for some slime-ball in a ski mask to hide back there, either. Get your priorities straight."

"They're straight." Her voice rose indignantly.

"Right. That's why hiding a drainpipe is more important than your safety."

The copper in her eyes glinted. "I want the front of my house to look nice. So sue me. But don't lecture me about priorites, Mr. Winning-Is-Everything. I know what's most important in life."

"Oh, excuse me. I guess snooping into a man's personal, financial and business affairs without his knowledge, then deliberately setting out to make him marry you—even if you don't love him—is more honorable than trying to succeed in business."

Flushing, she carefully lowered the hand cupping her towel turban. "I'm not particularly proud of what I'm doing, no."

"Then why do it?"

The pink in her cheeks deepened. "The ends will justify the means. Isn't that what you said when we halved the standard agency media commission to lock in the Toyota Dealership Group account?"

His ears heated. "Apples to oranges," he countered, repeating a favorite phrase of hers.

"Why? The Group was perfectly content with its agency of record until you offered a sweeter deal. You didn't do anything illegal, but it was marginally unethical. And in the end, the Group got a better creative product and more responsive service, right?"

"Yes, but that's—"

"In my case," she overrode his objection, "I know more about Larry's personal and business interests than the average woman, therefore I'm undercutting the competition with a marginally unethical advantage. But if our relationship goes anywhere, in the end he'll get a dedicated wife and loving mother to his children. Apples to apples," she finished smugly.

Thoughts of the relationship going anywhere that produced children twisted the snakes in his belly. "What about all that talk about soul mates, Lizzy? I thought you wanted the kind of marriage Travis and Kara have—not your mom and dad."

She winced. "Low blow."

Snakes had a tendency to strike low. "You don't need to undercut the competition, that's all I'm saying. Be patient. The next man you meet might be your soul mate, and the relationship will develop naturally. Forget about Sanderson."

Her expression grew strained. "What about Sky-

Hawk Airlines? Should I forget about helping you prepare for the presentation, too?''

He weighed the skeletal condition of the marketing plan against the image of Lizzy in Sanderson's arms.

''I'll flesh out the marketing plan from your existing notes. We'll tear up the damn contract. You sure don't need my help getting a date, that much is obvious.''

Looking more distressed than flattered, she gripped her robe tighter. ''I don't understand. We made a deal. Why are you trying to back out of it now?''

''I've had time to think it over, and I just want—'' Cameron stopped, unable to voice the dozen lascivious things he suddenly wanted from this remarkable woman.

Rising above them all, clean and pure of motive, was one thing he wanted for her.

''I just want you to be happy,'' he said from his heart.

Confusion and desperation swept over her face. ''Then don't tear up the contract. Please. I need your help tonight.''

Alarm shot through Cameron. He'd never seen her look so torn. ''What's wrong, honey?''

His endearment seemed only to increase her agitation. ''Nothing's *wrong*. But I could use your help putting together a decent meal. You're a much better cook than I am.''

''You want me to help you feed the dimwit,'' he said evenly.

''Stop calling him that. But…yes. And I want your advice about…something.''

God, he missed the days when she hadn't balked at everything he suggested. ''You're not gonna give up the game, are you?''

For an instant she appeared to waver, then her chin angled. ''I'm through playing it safe, if that's what you mean. You said you wanted me to be happy. I'm convinced this is my best shot.''

Sighing, he laid the clippers carefully on top of the ladder and turned to give her his full attention.

''All right, Lizzy, you win. What advice do you need about…something?''

CHAPTER TEN

ELIZABETH TRIED NOT to stare, but she'd never seen Cameron sweat before. Standing on the ladder, his dark gold hair a wet-seal brown at the temples and nape, his white shirt exposing a wedge of tanned, glistening chest, he looked hot, surprisingly rumpled…and very masculine.

She licked her dry lips. "I'm not sure what to do about after dinner, exactly."

Actually, she planned on playing with her new dog. Larry considered Elizabeth's acceptance of a needy animal fair trade for his cooperation in her plan.

"What, exactly, do you mean?" Cameron asked in a cautious tone.

"You know. I'm not sure what to do. With Larry, I mean."

He scowled. "Give him a mint and send him home."

Excellent. "I'm serious. I wasn't expecting to have a dinner date at home until at least the sixth date. The plan calls for liqueur of choice on the couch, followed by kissing, et cetera. On a second date, how much et cetera should I allow?''

"None," he said firmly. "Et cetera on the second date is a bad idea. Who wants to marry a slut? In fact, I'd limit the 'kissing' to a peck at the door when he leaves—which should be early, by the way. Tomorrow's a workday."

Her optimism screeched to a halt. "This is all a big joke to you, isn't it?"

"Do you see me laughing? Look, Sanderson is giving you the big rush now, but you need to slow things down and test the water, before you're in too deep to avoid getting hurt. I'm trying to *protect* you."

Her heart sank. "Well, stop trying. I don't want your protection."

"Tough. You've got it anyway. Your parents are too caught up in their own problems to look out for you. You've got no siblings. Consider me a surrogate big brother."

Oh, it was hopeless. He would never see her as anything but good ol' Lizzy. "I'm not a child, and I'm not your sister. If I *had* a brother, I wouldn't tolerate him interfering in my love life."

"You wouldn't have a choice. That's how it is in big families." He wiped a trickle of sweat from his forehead with one sleeve, pulling damp cotton taut over muscular shoulders. "Be careful what you wish for, Lizzy."

No truer words were ever spoken. She'd been fooling herself. He was beyond her reach.

"You want to protect me? Buy me a box of condoms. Telling me a man can't possibly be interested in me for a long-term relationship is not the kind of advice I wanted from you when you signed our contract."

No, Lizzy, men will get in line for the chance to share their life with you, her imagination answered.

"Condoms! You're joking, right?" Cameron said.

So.

Time to cut her losses and run. "For an eligible bachelor, you really are naive. I'm afraid the best thing all around is for us to forget that contract, like you said."

"You mean it?"

His hopeful expression cut her to the quick. He couldn't wait to get rid of the albatross around his neck.

"Yes," she snapped. "In fact, I think you should go home right now and tear it up."

"Right now?"

"The sooner the better!"

He frowned. "Why are you so mad?"

Stupid, clueless man! "I am not mad. I simply no longer want you here. Please leave."

"But…what about the bush?"

"The bonsai tree? Chop the sucker down, I don't care!"

"Well, hell. Why'd you come out here in the first place if you weren't checking on your drainpipe camouflage?"

Because she'd been as jumpy as a wet cat during her shower. Because she'd had to see his face, to hear his voice, to make sure he was really on a ladder near her garage, and not a figment of her imagination.

"Because there's a six-pack of Heineken and a pitcher of tea in the fridge. I came out here to see if you wanted something to drink."

"Oh." His forehead relaxed slightly. "Well... yeah. A beer would be great."

"Fine." She turned and stalked off across the driveway. "Get it yourself!" she called over her shoulder.

She was his employee, not his slave.

"Fine!" he bellowed. "And you're welcome. It was my pleasure risking my neck and ruining my clothes to keep you safe!"

She whirled around, one hand jerking up to catch the turban sliding over her ear. "On second thought, stay out of my six-pack, and keep your butchering hands off my cedar bush!"

"Like hell I will. It's comin' down before I leave, sister."

"If you were so worried about protecting me,

brother, you could've come over anytime in the past three years and cut it down. You had your chance. Don't touch that bush.''

In answer, he snatched the hedge clippers from the ladder, turned to the bush and began hacking away in earnest.

Despite her bare feet, she did a fair job of stomping forward on the cement.

''Stop that!'' she ordered.

Grunt-snip! Grunt-snip!

She shoved the ladder.

Dropping the clippers, he grappled for balance as aluminum wobbled, rattled and finally stilled.

With ominous calm, he climbed down to the grass, rolled his sleeves to midforearm, then hooked both thumbs in his hip pockets.

His glare was anything but calm.

An arm's length away, she glared back.

He blew out a breath. ''Are you crazy, or just PMSing?''

Her hackles rose. ''Are you deaf, or just terminally stupid? I repeat. Don't cut that bush.''

''Fine!''

''Good!'' She yanked the towel from her wet curls and draped it behind her neck. ''Now, if you'll excuse me, I'm going inside to dry my hair.''

''While you're in there, see if you can get your panties out of a wad, why don't you?''

She stiffened, then regally lifted her nose. "Must you resort to sophomoric gender slurs?"

"No. But they're much more satisfying than generic insults, so why would I resist?"

Her sophomoric tantrum returned. "I do *not* have my panties in a wad!"

"Could've fooled me."

"Ha! I already have. I'm not *wearing* any panties!"

Her triumphant announcement echoed in the still evening air.

Parents were home from work, kids were inside washing up before dinner, dogs were silent as the neighborhood settled down for the night. A dove cooed softly from somewhere close. A souped-up engine backfired once on a distant street.

But her focus had narrowed to startled tawny eyes that were wary and watchful, wondering and waiting…waiting…as if for a sign from her on how to proceed.

Elizabeth didn't know how her heart pumped so hard, since the rest of her was paralyzed.

When he finally spoke, his voice came from deep inside his chest. "Be sure you correct that little oversight before Sanderson gets here, okay?"

Disappointment stirred her limbs. "Still playing big brother?"

"Still being your friend."

Friend. Sister. Employee. Colleague. He was a

man, wasn't he? She would by damn make him see her as a woman just once in her life, if she had to strip naked to do it!

"Well, friend—" she lifted one end of the towel and flung it around her neck "—I'm feeling adventurous tonight. Maybe I won't correct the oversight. Maybe I'll go 'commando.' I've read that can be liberating for a woman who might otherwise feel awkward and inhibited on a date."

His burnished lashes lowered a fraction. He studied her inscrutably. "Interesting theory."

"Yes, I thought so. Apparently, even if a woman's companion never knows her little secret, *she* does, and that can make her feel a bit wicked, and act more…spontaneous." She gathered a robe lapel in each hand and snugged them close. "So I've read," she added.

"Spontaneity can be dangerous."

"You think so?"

His eyes glinted. "I know so."

"Hmm. Supposedly a little danger can also be quite liberating. For instance, the woman I spoke of earlier may or may not choose to divulge her 'wicked' secret to her companion at any time. Depending on where they are—and I've read that public places are particularly effective—she can allow him to share her heightened self-awareness."

What was he thinking? Impossible to tell. She

only knew she had his complete attention, and wanted to keep it.

"From what I've read, the experience is supposed to be very stimulating. I wouldn't know, of course." She lowered her lashes slowly, lifted them swiftly. "Would you?"

His jaw bulged once. The fingers outside his pockets curled up.

Narrowing his eyes, he tilted his head. "What are you trying to prove, Lizzy? That you can be wicked and sexy? That you can tease with the best of 'em? That you can get even your friend hot and bothered?"

Every word was a lash to her conscience, another humiliation to bear.

"Well, guess what, friend?" he asked.

Shaking her head, she lowered her hands and started to back away.

In the blink of an eye he reached out and grabbed her robe lapels. "You can."

He yanked her powerfully to his body and up to her toes. There was no trace of friend, boss or colleague in his thrillingly fierce gaze.

At last...at last...at last!

She'd staged this scene endlessly in her imagination, rehearsed it with pillows a hundred times as a teen, honed her skills as an adult in a series of amateur productions with lackluster understudies— all in order to ready herself for her big break.

But she wasn't prepared.

The blinding white-gold heat of Cameron's stare was more awesome than Broadway spotlights. She'd put that smolder of passion in his eyes.

His features were taut, his focus scorching, his intent unmistakable as he effortlessly lifted her another half inch. "Lizzy," he said in a strange guttural voice. "What are you doing to me?"

Even her bulky robe and knotted belt couldn't disguise the evidence of at least one thing she'd managed to do to him.

At last…at last…at last!

She had mere seconds to exult before his head swooped down, obliterating coherent thought.

The shock of pleasure that zapped to her dangling toes threatened to singe the grass beneath. His mouth was firm but mobile. Warm and skilled and intoxicatingly ravenous. He ate at her lips with gentle bites and moist suckling, tugging at her innards and making her head spin.

She groped for something solid, found his shoulders, dug her fingers into bunched muscle and opened her mouth for a deeper kiss.

His hot, wet plunge would have buckled her knees had he not already held her up.

He swept her sleek interior with succulent abandon, as if he were frantic to learn her texture and taste, as if he liked what he was learning. Liked it so much he couldn't get enough. At her first tentative stroke in return, he made a gruff noise of pleasure and drew her tongue into his mouth.

She tasted the salt of his recent labor and an unfamiliar, altogether delicious essence she knew instinctively was his alone.

She liked it. Liked it so much she went delving for more. And more and more and more. Fifteen years of curiosity and lonely fantasy fueled her questing exploration. Her inhibitions fell away.

Sliding her fingers into thick hair damp with sweat, she hummed her lusty appreciation low in her throat.

The sound galvanized him into a quick spin.

Without breaking contact with her mouth, he lowered her only long enough to clamp his hands behind her lower spine, then lift and carry her forward, her feet bobbling against his shins.

When her shoulder blades met a solid rough surface, he lowered her slowly until her feet were flat. The kiss became desperate. A mesh of tongues and teeth that aroused but didn't satisfy.

Nudging her knees and the lower half of her robe apart, he crowded closer.

She arched to receive him, the knotted belt at her waist a minor discomfort, the ridged length straining his zipper and pressing her belly a tantalizing tease. Wriggling didn't help.

Tilting her pelvis, she eased him into a long slide downward that broke the kiss and wrung a sweet groan from them both. He stopped exactly where she ached the most.

"Oh, man," he said thickly, his breath beating hard and fast in her ear. "I was afraid of something like this."

Drugged on passion, Elizabeth didn't know where she was, much less what he meant.

She opened heavy eyelids and saw a rusty drainpipe on her left. Those were bricks supporting her back, then. They stood in the spicy dark shelter provided by the thick cedar bush.

"Tell me to stop, Lizzy. Please."

She worked an arm up between their bodies, slipped her hand inside his shirt, and scored her fingernails over damp skin and silken hair.

"No," she said, fascinated with his hard muscular chest. Again she hummed her approval.

Again the sound triggered a dramatic response.

In a single swift move he reared back, jerked open the top of her robe and peeled terry cloth over her shoulders, trapping her arms at her sides. Seemingly helpless to prevent the movement, he thrust his hips once, then lowered his head to trace her collarbone with the tip of his tongue.

Icy hot shivers avalanched down the slopes of her breasts to the sensitive nipples barely covered by cloth.

"Tell me to stop," Cameron whispered hoarsely against her skin.

But she was incapable of speech, lost in splendor.

His mouth moved on to the base of her throat, where his tongue lapped and swirled the hollow for every last drop of whatever fed his wondrous ardor. Her eyelids drifted shut.

When her head lolled back against brick his tongue quickened, mimicking her wildly fluttering pulse, conjuring images of an act she'd never experienced but suddenly imagined in vivid detail. Liquid heat sluiced straight downward, and she grew conscious of fabric against her naked flesh.

Shyness crept into her passion. She opened her eyes, increasingly embarrassed.

She'd wanted him to treat her like a desirable woman, someone worthy of pursuit, a challenge he couldn't resist. Instead, she was backed against a wall next to a drainpipe like an alleyway prostitute!

Struggling to pull her robe closed, she succeeded only in dislodging his mouth. He raised his head, and she increased her efforts.

Seconds later, his unnatural stillness penetrated her brain. She looked down at herself in dismay. The erect tip of her left breast had popped free of terry cloth to point up at his riveted gaze.

"Stop," she said weakly.

His short laugh was incredulous and strained.

Oh, no, her dusky flesh quivered with every heartbeat. Mortifyingly turgid. Horrifyingly exposed. "Let me cover myself."

"No, no, no," he crooned, moving back just enough to palm her breast. "Your body is beautiful, Lizzy. Don't you know that? So soft—" a flick of his thumb made her gasp "—so responsive. You're making me crazy. Don't tell me to stop. Not yet. Please, Lizzy. Not yet."

The enormity of the moment struck her.

That was Cameron's voice begging hoarsely for her favors, his timber wolf eyes gleaming in the fading light. She lowered her gaze to the tanned fingers kneading her pale flesh, and a rush of sensuality washed away her shyness.

"All right," she whispered.

His hand tightened almost painfully, then relaxed.

When he plucked her nipple to full rigid attention, she closed her eyes on the sight and let sensation take over. His hand was large and warm, his fingers exquisitely gentle. He cupped her full weight and lifted, creating a mound she sensed he would put to good use.

She waited breathlessly, her anticipation building.

The rasp of his beard-roughened cheek jerked her eyes open.

Looking up from her plumped flesh, he growled his approval, the masculine equivalent of her earlier hum.

The sound reached deep inside her and stroked something elemental. She reached for his face.

Skimming a fingertip from the pulse rapping at his temple to the curve beneath his cheekbone to the strong clean line of his jaw, she gripped his chin and guided him firmly where she wanted.

He might've chuckled, but she couldn't be sure, because all her senses had pooled in one location.

O-o-oh…that magical tongue.

Warm and wet, it circled the target ever and ever closer, leaving a damp trail for the evening air to chill, puckering a nipple already taut and beaded. When at last he drew her into his mouth, his upper teeth slicing just short of pain, she shuddered and fisted her hands in his hair.

The moist hot tugs at her breast pulled spasms of desire through her pliant body. Inarticulate sounds came from her throat. She stood the torturous ecstasy as long as she could, then pulled his head up by his hair.

"Jeez—"

Her lips stopped his protest. Flattening her palms over his ears, she told him with her kiss what she'd never dared to say out loud. *I adore the boy you were. I love the man you became. I cherish the man you could be.*

His arms came around her hard in a crushing embrace, and for one glorious moment, his kiss was more emotion than skill.

When he tore his mouth free, she chased his lips, bereft and confused.

"Shh!" he warned, head cocked, body tensed.

A car rumbled slowly past the front of her house, windows open, music blaring. "Check out the Jaguar, man. Is your neighbor rich or somethin'?"

"That's not her car," Miguel's faint voice answered. "Belongs to that guy I told you about—the one loaning me a Rocket Sock for my ankle. Maybe he brought it. Let me out here and I'll see."

At Elizabeth's panic-stricken look, Cameron stepped back, pulled her robe up and together, and spoke in her ear. "It's in the back seat of my car. Wait till I distract him, then go inside."

He smoothed his hair, looked down at the front of his pants with a grimace, and yanked his long shirttail out.

A car door slammed. "Thanks for the ride, dude. See ya."

As the engine roared off, Cameron slipped around the bush and scooped up the fallen hedge clippers. "Hey, Miguel! I thought that was you."

"Hey, Cameron! Man, what'd you do to Elizabeth's bush?"

"Reserve your judgment for after I finish the job, okay, wise guy?"

He'd led Miguel to her left and stood near the sidewalk, where the bush would hide her escape from view. As their voices droned on, Elizabeth slunk on wobbly legs to her front door.

How he managed to sound so normal, when she was so shattered she could barely turn a doorknob, was a mystery.

Slipping inside her house, she refused to contemplate the logical explanation.

That the major earthquake she'd just experienced had only been a minor ripple in Cameron's life.

CHAPTER ELEVEN

AT THREE O'CLOCK ON FRIDAY, Cameron sat at the head of the conference room table and waited for Lizzy to show up for the staff meeting. She'd specifically requested they convene an hour earlier than usual, to accommodate her new strategic recommendations, and she was late. Again.

His stress level, which had merely been dizzyingly high before he'd climbed a ladder three days ago, was rapidly approaching outer space. His deflector shields wouldn't hold much longer.

If he didn't get control of the situation soon, he would either burn to a crisp, or hit zero gravity and go floating off to a world bounded by padded walls.

As the rest of the SkyHawk account team settled in chairs, hauling out notes and chatting, Cameron doodled idly in the margin of his legal pad.

Tomorrow night at the ADDY Awards, he would have to play gracious host not only to Carol, whom he'd made a point to remind Lizzy was his date, but also to his entire family and Sanderson!

When she'd asked if Cameron's invitation to the awards ceremony still stood, he hadn't known she wanted to bring along the dimwit until after he'd said yes. She was still playing her dangerous game.

Bearing down hard on his ballpoint pen, he added a second horn to the devil's face he'd drawn.

Jeez. He'd been suckered by the oldest feminine trick in the book! She was using another man to try to make him jealous. Sanderson had never been her true target, Cameron now knew. Any doubts on that score had been put to rest behind her cedar bush. He was the man she'd set out to win from the first!

Not that he'd known that when she'd flirted so suggestively about her little secret. He'd simply thought she was testing her feminine wiles on the nearest available male.

So he'd wanted to prove a point, to show her that a man's libido was separate from his more tender emotions, and dangerous for a rookie to control. He'd intended to make her think twice before throwing her curves at a less experienced player in the future. He'd hoped to make her give up the game.

Instead, at the first touch of those dainty plump lips, he'd acted like a kid begging his date to advance to home base.

Lord God above, she'd tasted sweet! And sinfully spontaneous. No previous experience had prepared him for the blend of passion, tenderness and trust he'd sensed in her mind-blowing kiss.

Sex would never be casual to Lizzy—or with

Lizzy. A temporary fling was out of the question. Miguel's interruption was a blessing in disguise, Cameron had realized as she'd slipped inside her house unseen, and relatively untouched.

He'd been so rattled by his lack of control, he'd given Miguel the promised Rocket Sock, then promptly driven home...to toss and turn and remember how good and right it had felt to have and to hold Lizzy during those incredible moments.

How the hell could he know if his feelings would last a lifetime? His record so far was only six dates.

"I'm sorry, I'm sorry," Lizzy apologized loudly from the conference room doorway.

His focus cleared on yellow-lined paper. He'd drawn a circle of hearts around the devil's face. Jeez.

Looking up, he watched her walk in her familiar navy pantsuit to her usual chair and settle in with her normal efficient movements, and experienced extraordinary pleasure at the ordinary sight.

He suddenly noticed that Joel, Pete, Susan and Mitch were staring at him curiously. Je-e-ez.

Cameron leaned back, pulling his pad to the edge of the table and said without preamble, "Jim called today with the schedule."

Everyone's attention sharpened. They'd all been waiting to learn the confirmed date of their Sky-Hawk presentation, hoping for an extra weekend of preparation time.

"Three weeks from today," Cameron announced grimly. "Ad Ventures presents at nine that morning. We're scheduled for three o'clock."

Groans and protests broke out all around.

"It's bad enough we get stuck with the siesta slot after lunch," Pete grumbled. "But on Friday? They'll be thinking about their weekend plans, and want us to wrap up fast."

"No, they won't." Lizzy's calm assurance drew every eye. "You'll all be so brilliant and inspiring, they'll have a million questions afterward. It happens every time."

Yet she'd never witnessed the phenomenon, Cameron realized, struck with remorse and shame. He'd never encouraged her to overcome her fear of public speaking. She'd never experienced the incomparable thrill of watching her hard work received with respect and enthusiasm.

Tim stopped fiddling with his Palm Pilot. "Before I set this appointment in stone, any chance of you rescheduling for another day, Cameron?"

Mitch shot the account supervisor a disgruntled look. "Afraid you might have to actually work past five o'clock like the rest of us?"

Three times a week, Tim blew out the door so Ginger could make her six-o'clock Tae Bo exercise class while he baby-sat.

"Hey, buddy—" Tim thrust out his chin "—where were you at nine o'clock last night, huh?

I came back here to write up job orders and fill in time sheets. See, I don't get to stay in the office and do my paperwork on the company clock. I'm out there fighting traffic to get to clients so I can fight some more, explaining why the ad they paid for doesn't contain information they specifically told me to put in—all because you decided it would clutter the design or taint the creative integrity!''

Mitch sneered. ''Would you like some more cheese with that whine? Pete, Joel and I worked here till eleven Wednesday night on the Texas Telco annual report design and copy you promised them in a week—without checking the jobs scheduled ahead of it first!''

''Are you kidding? The creative department is always behind schedule. Maybe if you'd grow up and quit playing practical jokes, you'd have more time to—'

''Enough!'' Cameron boomed, causing startled flinches.

He collected himself and continued in a calmer tone. ''Look, I know everyone's putting in extra hours and nerves are frazzled. But complaining and bickering is self-destructive. Friday was the only full day Gary Matthews had open that worked for everyone involved. Jim called Ad Ventures first, and they jumped on the morning time. End of story. Let's deal with the situation and move forward.''

He eyed Mitch and Tim sternly. ''You two are

going to quit sniping at each other, starting now, before the rest of us kill you.''

"Thank you, Lord," Susan said, looking heavenward.

"Amen," Pete added.

Joel cast a droll look Cameron's way. "You can always put 'em in 'time out' for fifteen minutes. That usually shapes up my kids for at least a couple of hours."

Everyone but the culprits chuckled.

"Very funny," Tim said, reaching into a briefcase near his feet. "Take a look at this, and then tell me I'm being unreasonable."

He yanked out an easel-backed picture frame, rose halfway from his chair and stretched over the table to hand it to Cameron.

At first glance, nothing seemed amiss with the family portrait.

Two little girls, daughters from Tim's first marriage, sat on a white carpet, their black velvet skirts billowing, their hands folded demurely in their laps. Behind them on a red velvet love seat, Ginger wore a long white slinky gown that showed off the results of her Tae Bo class. Tim's black turtleneck and slacks were a perfect foil for his eight-month-old son, dressed all in white and perched on his knee.

Cameron peered closer beneath the baby's tiny white baseball cap.

Mitch's bearded face grinned back.

With tremendous effort, Cameron kept his expression bland and looked up at Tim. "I guess I'd lose my sense of humor, too, if my baby were this butt ugly."

In the stunned silence, Tim guffawed.

Mitch scowled.

Grinning, Cameron turned the portrait around, popped out the easel back and stood the frame where everyone could see. Joel snorted first. Susan hooted next. Soon everyone was laughing and jostling for a closer look at the ludicrous picture.

After a few minutes, Cameron intervened. "Okay, people, recess is over. Mitch, after the meeting, return the original portrait, and stay away from everyone's personal property from now on. Understood?"

"Yeah, boss. Sorry."

Cameron nodded, silently thanking Photoshop software and the agency's new color printer for inspiring Mitch's latest prank. The earlier tension in the room was gone.

He scanned the relaxed, attentive faces. "Elizabeth asked for a little extra time today, because she's developed some new recommendations that might alter our current creative direction. Let's keep an open mind and hear her out."

Meeting grateful brown eyes, he nodded. "The floor's all yours."

"Thanks, Cameron." She pulled a manila file

folder closer, flipped it open and drew a deep breath. "As you all know, I'm leaving Malloy Marketing after the SkyHawk presentation."

Cameron stiffened. What was this about?

"It was a big decision, and has made me realize that for years, I never challenged my safe and familiar patterns of thinking. I basically stayed the same person. My life strategy wasn't Playing To Win. It was Playing Not To Lose. There's a big difference."

Cameron glanced around at his colleagues' compassionate interest. Even Mitch's cynical expression had softened.

"I did a little research on the subject—" she held up a palm and smiled self-mockingly "—yes, I know that comes as a huge surprise."

When the chuckles faded, she continued. "Playing Not To Lose is an avoidance strategy driven by fear. Most commonly, fear of being wrong, fear of failure, fear of rejection, or fear of feeling awkward and looking foolish.

"If you're wondering what the heck this has to do with SkyHawk Airlines, I'll tell you."

Cameron was as hooked as the others. She'd captivated her audience within thirty seconds.

Not bad for a poor public speaker.

"We're allocating huge sums of money for traditional broadcast and print media. We're stressing competitive price, convenient flight schedules and superior service in our launch campaign.

"There's not a thing wrong with our current strategy. It's familiar and based on sound marketing principles. It won't be a huge failure in the marketplace, or be rejected by the client, or called foolish by industry analysts."

Her pause had them all straining forward. "By the same token, it won't reap huge market share, profits or industry praise, either."

"We're entering an established, mature market, not a growth market," Tim pointed out. "Huge gains are virtually impossible."

"'Virtually' is the key word." She smiled slowly. "Dozens of case studies prove that fearless entrepreneurs and innovative thinkers can achieve what was thought impossible by traditional marketers."

Her gaze turned hazy, and off she went. "In 1984, the Harley-Davidson company was on the verge of bankruptcy. The motorcycle industry laughed at Clyde Fessler's HOG club for Harley-Davidson owners. But he knew his customers, and created a unique community for them. Today, HOG has over three hundred fifty thousand members and a thousand chapters around the world, and the company reported over two billion dollars in revenues. The ad budget was less than two million."

Cameron noted the startled looks around the table, especially Susan's.

"The National Basketball Association, and its teams, were virtually ignored by this country when David Stern took over as commissioner. But he saw basketball as a balletic, action-packed sport tailor-made for television, and consciously decided to market its athletes as heroes and entertainers.

"He forged alliances with sponsors like Nike, Reebok, Coca-Cola and McDonald's, and got hundreds of millions of dollars' worth of marketing goodwill without spending a nickel of the NBA's money. He was the first to market a sports league as a brand—"

"Elizabeth," Cameron interrupted. "Stop. Focus. SkyHawk Airlines?"

She smiled sheepishly, then grew serious and looked at each one of them in turn. "I believe we're so afraid of botching this opportunity for the agency, that we're Playing Not To Lose instead of Playing To Win. I believe we're doing the client, and ourselves, an injustice by proposing our current strategy."

"Wait a minute," Pete blurted. "I'm sorry, but everyone in this room is competitive, and nobody plays to win harder than Cameron."

"I'll second that," Mitch said, his eyes amused. "He damn near killed me the year Malloy Marketing fielded an intramural softball team. Be glad you didn't work here then, Pete. The man had us practicing four nights a week.''

Cameron cocked a brow. ''And when we won the league tournament, I seem to recall you crowing the loudest.''

Mitch grinned reminiscently. ''Yeah, it was sweet. But beating Ad Ventures for the SkyHawk account would be much sweeter.''

Lizzy didn't smile. ''First of all, when I use the term Playing To Win, it has nothing to do with 'beating' someone else, or making someone else 'lose.'

''It means that when we want something, whether it's the SkyHawk account or a new house or a better relationship—whatever our goal or dream is—we go for it with everything we've got. We push ourselves to the limit, with no fear for what we might lose. And maybe we make mistakes, or look stupid, or get rejected, or fail big time...''

Just thinking about it squeezed Cameron's lungs in a familiar fist of fear.

''...but if so, we're a little wiser for it. A little better prepared for the next challenge. We've pushed our limits and grown. We're not the same. It's a personal strategy. A life strategy, that's shared by most entrepreneurs and innovative thinkers. People like Clyde Fessler and David Stern.''

''And Gary Matthews,'' Susan said musingly.

''Exactly! He's the P. T. Barnum of the Las Vegas hotel and casino industry, and analysts are predicting he'll fall flat in his new venture. After all, others with more experience in the transportation industry have failed.

"Even his own marketing managers seem afraid his vision of what an airplane trip should be will spell disaster for the carrier's success. They're trying to keep him—and the ad agency they select—inside conventional boundaries. I say, let's break out. No guts, no glory."

Her excitement was as contagious as her rebellion against walls they'd all banged into repeatedly over the years.

"I say, let's take advantage of Gary's life strategy and think outside the box. Forget what makes his managers comfortable, or makes Malloy Marketing money, and sit in the traditional airline passenger seat with me for a minute."

She made a production out of leaning back and adopting a stiff position. "It's cramped and my neck hurts. I asked the flight attendant fifteen minutes ago for a blanket, but she got stopped by four other passengers and forgot about me. The food is awful. The movie's old and the headsets are uncomfortable. There's a cranky kid behind me and a three-hundred-pound linebacker beside me, using my armrest.

"The ticket price was competitive, because the

airlines monitor each other hourly and adjust their prices accordingly.

But I would've gladly paid more money…to have more fun.'' Relaxing, she grinned and waited.

Cameron was the first to bite. ''Fun?''

She nodded eagerly. ''Gary Matthews may not know the transportation business, but he's an expert in the business of making people pay gladly to have a good time.''

Looking around at the assembled team, Cameron saw the same fire-in-the-gut excitement on their faces he was experiencing for the first time in far too long. He spoke for them all.

''We're intrigued. What did you have in mind?''

ELIZABETH DRAINED HER LAST SIP of coffee, set the china cup in its saucer and twisted in her chair to search the crowded banquet room.

People were almost finished with dessert. The video presentation would begin soon. And of course, not a one of the harried waiters who'd served over two hundred ADDY Award guests was in sight.

A hand settled on her bare arm. She turned, almost bumped noses with Larry, jerked back and laughed self-consciously. ''Sorry.''

''Don't be. I'll rub noses with you anytime.'' His hazel eyes were warm, his tone intimate. He slid his palm up and down her arm once.

She flushed, confused and uncomfortable. From the moment her "date" had picked her up at home, his attentiveness and attraction to her had seemed very real, and she wasn't quite certain what to do about it.

"Were you looking for a waiter just now? Is there something you'd like?"

She wasn't used to her every nuance being interpreted. "Yes. I was hoping to get more coffee before the lights dim."

He squeezed her arm. "You got it."

Dropping his napkin beside his dessert plate, Larry scooted his chair backward, then rose. "Anyone else need a coffee refill, or maybe something from the bar?" he asked politely.

Conversations around the table paused.

Looking up en masse, the Malloys were a dazzling sight to behold—none more so than Cameron. He seemed born to wear a tuxedo. The black and white starkness made his hair gleam like polished ingots, his tan seem a shade darker. He looked urbane and sophisticated without a trace of effeteness.

Eyeing the stunning blonde sitting beside him, Elizabeth admitted dismally to herself that Carol fit right into the family.

"I'd adore some coffee, Larry," Nancy said, her lovely gray eyes appreciative. "How thoughtful of you to ask."

Her husband John winced at the slight to his gallantry. Though his dark hair was turning silver, he was lean, fit and virile. The mold from which four extraordinarily handsome sons were cast.

Picking up his cue, Travis turned to his very beautiful, very pregnant blond wife. "Honey, would you like more decaf?"

"No, but I'd like the rest of your cheesecake, if you're finished. Vowing to love me in sickness and in health includes prenatal weight gain. Postpartum, too," she added quickly, her laughing green eyes meeting his.

What Elizabeth saw in Travis's brown gaze made her cheeks heat and a pang of envy stab her heart.

"Jeez," Cameron said to no one in particular. He shoved back from the table and stood. "I'll handle the bar orders, Sanderson. You want anything?"

"No thanks." Larry rested a hand on Elizabeth's nape and massaged gently. "If you're sure you don't need me to help, I'll go see if I can find a waiter with fresh coffee."

For an instant, Cameron's sophisticated golden veneer vanished. His eyes hardened to tempered brass. "I don't need you."

The fingers on Elizabeth's nape tightened.

Silverware clinked and voices babbled at other tables. No one in her immediate vicinity seemed to breathe.

"Why'd everybody get so quiet?" Carol asked loudly, breaking the tension. She'd had four glasses of wine with dinner, growing more touchy-feely with each one.

Kara and Nancy began chatting brightly to fill the silence.

Larry looked down at Elizabeth with a tight smile. "Excuse me, please."

With a parting nod to the other women, he wove through the maze of tables toward double doors across the room.

"I'll take a beer, Cam," Jake piped up on Elizabeth's left.

Some of the rigidity left Cameron's body. "Seth, Dad? Last call."

"No thanks, son."

Seth gave a negative wave, his dark blue eyes keen and thoughtful.

Cameron started to turn.

"Wait!" Carol rose a bit unsteadily and claimed possession of his arm. "I'll go with you. Do you think they have a decent cognac in this place?"

His mouth thinned. "I think you're in no shape to notice the difference." As he pulled her away from the table, she laughed her hyena laugh.

He could tell her to drop dead, and she'd no doubt act as if he'd said something terribly witty.

Elizabeth stared at bumpy vertebrae and jutting shoulder blades in a strapless red designer gown, and assured herself the front side would've been just as malnourished without skilled medical intervention.

"Well, hallelujah," Seth said in his slow, deliberate way.

"There is a God," Jake agreed reverently.

She snapped to attention. Six pairs of eyes stared at her wonderingly, as if she were a beloved child who'd displayed unexpected cleverness.

"Hot damn!" Travis slapped his palms together and rubbed briskly. "It's payback time! Who would've believed?"

"Travis. Hon." Kara patted her husband's shoulder. "I love you for not noticing, but have you really looked at Elizabeth tonight?"

He blinked.

"I have!" Jake said enthusiastically.

"Me, too." Although quieter, Seth's tone was just as admiring.

Nancy cut her eyes up at John. "You might as well admit it, too."

His face grew ruddy. "I'm old, but I'm not blind."

Elizabeth's mouth slackened as the four men eyed her with frank appreciation and broke into trademark crooked grins. She grabbed her glass of water and took a gulp.

"Hey, Travis, did you see when Larry rubbed her

neck?'' Jake chortled. ''Cameron almost ripped off the guy's arm!''

''Yeah, was that rich, or what? Elizabeth, if I lay a big kiss on you in front of Cameron, don't slug me, okay? It's for a good cause.''

She looked wildly at his wife.

Kara shrugged. ''It's a long story. I flung myself at Cameron and kissed him in a nightclub once, and Travis has never forgiven him.''

''He enjoyed it too damn much,'' Travis grumbled without malice.

''Settle down, everyone, or we'll scare the poor girl away.'' Nancy turned to Elizabeth, her eyes growing misty. ''Don't let Cameron scare you, either, Elizabeth. He's being stubborn, like all the Malloys. But I promise you, he's worth the patience you've shown all these years.''

All these years?

Nancy leaned into John, who circled an arm around her shoulders and hugged her close. Travis did the same to Kara. Seth and Jake smiled encouragingly.

Elizabeth swallowed hard, her gratitude struggling with dismay. The Malloy family had seen her with Cameron maybe a dozen times during the past ten years. ''Was I that obvious?''

They looked at each other and sobered.

John spoke first, wearing his patriarch hat. ''Not to anyone who wasn't looking for the signs, honey.

We waited, and hoped he would come to his senses, and that you two would wind up together. Quite frankly, I'd about given up.''

Gratitude won out. Their warm and boisterous support made her feel a part of the family. Her throat thickened. ''In case you hadn't noticed, Cameron and I are a long way from being together tonight.''

''Oh, we noticed,'' Kara said, casting a conspiratorial look around the table. ''But I'm sure something could be arranged about that...if you're game.''

Elizabeth had seen Cameron's face, too. He was in no mood for more games. No guts, no glory.

It was time to Play To Win. ''I'm game.''

Green eyes took on a catlike gleam. ''Show everyone your purse, Elizabeth.''

Her purse? Actually, it was Rachel's, but Elizabeth didn't quibble. She scooped a small black satin clutch with rhinestone-studded clasp from the floor and held it aloft.

Kara raised her own black satin clutch, identical but for the shape of the clasp, and smiled serenely. ''That's what I thought. Isn't it lucky that we both have great taste?''

CHAPTER TWELVE

CAMERON PLANTED his right knee in the dirt, parted fragrant branches and peered carefully through Lizzy's cedar bush. If his brothers ever found out what he was doing now, he'd have to shoot them. Or himself.

Their teasing would be merciless, relentless and a fate worse than prison or death.

He glared at the poorly lit front porch and willed the dimwit to appear. Long minutes passed, while the snakes in his belly hissed and writhed and poisoned his seething blood.

This was worse than spying that time at Chuy's Restaurant. Much worse. A thousand times worse. If he had a shred of decency or self-respect, he would get up and walk away.

His left knee joined his right in the dirt. Stabilized, he leaned forward and studied the large front window closer. What were they doing behind those closed mini blinds? Allowing 'et cetera' to take its natural course?

He'd purposefully backed off from Lizzy following their steamy kiss, thinking himself noble, thinking her infatuated and vulnerable, thinking he should be absolutely certain she could count on him before he made the next move.

In the meantime, he'd kept his date with Carol. So Lizzy had made another one with Sanderson, who was rich and successful. Who loved kids and animals and picnics. Who, far from backing off, seemed more smitten with each hour spent in her company. Tonight, Sanderson had openly staked his claim.

And Cameron, stuck with a woman he didn't want, had been forced to watch a rival woo the one he did.

He ground his teeth at the memory, wishing he could turn back the clock and ask Lizzy to the awards ceremony as his date. The only thing being noble had done was give her the wrong impression. Maybe drive her into Sanderson's arms. She might've decided a bird in hand was better than a two-timing snake behind the bush.

Cameron released the parted branches. They snapped together with a violence that matched his mood.

He shouldn't have grabbed the flimsy excuse to come here. She'd obviously had a spare house key hidden someplace. Yet he'd accepted Jake's offer to drive Carol home, then broken speed limits to get here close on Sanderson's tail.

Seeing the Porsche in her driveway and the lights

on in the den, he'd parked a half block down the street. Midway to her house, he'd realized his prized Jaguar filled with eleven gold, three silver and one bronze ADDY Awards was unlocked.

He hadn't turned back.

He'd crept into her empty backyard, confirming that the two weren't waiting there for a locksmith. A bark from inside had taken a year off his life. Jeez. He'd actually forgotten about her new dog! It had taken all his willpower to keep from pressing his nose against the only window offering a view through open mini blinds. Instead, he'd slunk behind this bush.

Real friggin' chivalrous.

Where was his honor? Where was his courage? His father and brother had risked rejection to claim their women.

If he didn't do the same, he was worse than a snake. He was no better than a spineless worm squirming in the dirt.

Cameron patted the bulging pocket of his tuxedo jacket. He would walk up to the front door, boldly knock, hand Lizzy the purse, and see which "target" she sent home first. That's what he would do. He was a man, not a worm. He would jump the dimwit's claim. Yeah.

In a minute.

Instantly, his brothers' jeers and chicken clucks echoed in his mind.

Jeez. Resigned and resolved, he crawled from the circle of soil surrounding the bush onto stubbly grass.

The front door creaked open.

Damn.

He scrambled back onto the dirt, rose on his knees and leaned forward, parting thick branches. Nope. He squirmed for a clear view. Ah, better.

Sanderson had stepped out on the porch. He turned to face the door. Lizzy stood in the threshold, bending down to hold a golden retriever's collar. The dog strained forward, whining excitedly.

"Bye-bye, Lucy," Sanderson crooned, stooping over to stroke her reddish gold head. "You be a good girl and watch out for your new master, hear? She's very special."

Lizzy smiled. "You've been wonderful about all this, Larry. I don't know how I can ever thank you."

He looked up at the lovely face so close to his.

Don't do it, you bastard.

Sanderson stretched over the dog and claimed his thank-you.

Watching the lingering kiss, Cameron's grip on the branches grew tighter and tighter. He wanted to throw back his head and howl his pain and rage. He wanted to tear the dimwit apart with his bare hands. He wanted to—

Crack!

Damn. Thrashing his way free of scratchy cedar fronds, he heard frantic barking, and froze. Anger converted to panic.

He wanted to run like hell before they saw him!

"Who's there?" Sanderson called threateningly.

Cameron gathered his feet beneath him for the long sprint to his car.

"Lucy, no!" Lizzy shouted.

He sprang up just as a blur of motion rounded the bush.

Lucy rammed into his knees, toppling him backward. His head hit the grass with jarring force. Dazed, he braced himself for the feel of teeth sinking into flesh.

A warm tongue savagely assaulted his face.

Scrunching up his eyes and mouth, he turned his head and shoved the affectionate watchdog away. She surged right back.

"Cameron? Is that you?"

He endured Lizzy's incredulous tone philosophically.

Yes, this was the single most ignominious moment he'd ever experienced, besting his brothers' worst humiliations by a mile. But he'd be dead soon and wouldn't care. He was going to shoot himself at the first opportunity.

Someone hauled Lucy off his chest. He had a pretty good idea who, and kept his eyes closed.

"My, God, Malloy. Haven't you mutilated Elizabeth's poor cedar bush enough?'' Sanderson's annoyed tone was tinged with amusement.

Jeez.

Cameron opened his eyes and pushed himself into a sitting position. In the dark, the three figures were indistinct, but recognizable. Lizzy stood to his left. Sanderson restrained Lucy by her collar a foot to Cameron's right.

"I'm assuming you have a good explanation for being here," Lizzy said. "Why don't you share it with us?''

Fortunately, she hadn't specified "here" as this exact spot. She could've meant "here at my house."

Rising stiffly, Cameron fumbled in his jacket pocket and pulled out the evening bag. "I brought your purse. Your keys were in it, and I figured you might need them to get inside the house. But I guess you had a spare hidden someplace."

"Yes." She paused. "A phone call would've told you that, and saved you a trip."

He thought rapidly. "You've got Kara's purse, don't you?"

"Yes. I...picked it up by mistake. It's almost the same as mine. I was going to return it tomorrow before she left the hotel."

"She needs it tonight."

"She needs lipstick, powder and a comb?"

Cameron's face heated. Oh, what a tangled web...

Sanderson snorted. "I'll put Lucy in the backyard and let you two hash this out. Elizabeth, thanks again for a lovely evening. And congratulations to both of you for winning so many awards. You obviously are a talented team. Good night."

Lizzy murmured something polite.

Cameron mumbled something he promptly forgot.

He waited tensely as Sanderson pulled Lucy with him and coaxed her into the fenced yard. The gate clattered shut. Seconds later his car door opened and closed. The motor roared, then settled into a quiet purr. Headlights beamed at the garage.

Twelve feet away, in the deep night shadows behind the bush, black satin came to life and took on luscious shape. All pretense of nonchalance vanished as Cameron stared at Lizzy's dress.

The top half fit like a corset, cinching in her small waist and plumping her breasts. Spaghetti straps skimmed graceful white shoulders. Sleek satin flowed over her hips. The waterfall of fabric stopped two inches above her knees. Every man tonight had ogled those showgirl legs in sheer black stockings when she'd walked by. Her black netting underskirt kicked up flirtatiously with every step, completing the fantasy. His fantasy, anyway. The heavy heat building in his loins left no doubt of that.

The Porsche backed slowly out of the driveway. Black satin blended gradually into the night. Only her bare skin remained visible as a pale, almost ethereal glow.

"Did you really drive all the way to my house just to get Kara's purse?" Melodic and knowing, Lizzy's voice caressed him like a breeze.

"No."

"I'm assuming you have a good explanation. Why don't you share the truth with me this time?"

He'd spent his whole life conforming to the image of a confident winner, a man to be admired. Confessions of weakness didn't come easily. "You know why I came."

"I've learned the hard way not to make assumptions. Were you hiding back here?"

Where was a gun when a worm needed one? "Yes."

"Why?"

"After we kissed the other day, I thought..."

"You thought what, Cameron?"

No point in trying to wriggle out of the truth. "I got the impression you wanted me. Me, not Sanderson. I had to come here tonight and see if I was right, or wrong. And then when I got here, and you were already inside, I waited for him to leave. Only he didn't. He didn't.'' The intolerable memory rushed back, inciting the same turbulent emotions. Confusion and pain thickened his voice. "And the longer he stayed inside, the more convinced I was that he was making love to you."

She hesitated, then said carefully, "He was playing fetch with Lucy."

"I thought he was playing with you! I thought you'd changed your mind about me, and I couldn't breathe." His chest constricted on cue. "I pictured him touching you, Lizzy, and—God, it..."

"Hurt?"

"Yes!" The raw sound embarrassed him.

"Oh, Cameron."

He'd never inspired that particular tone in a woman's voice, and he didn't like it. Not one bit.

"I'm so sorry," she said, rubbing salt in his wounded ego.

Jeez. "I don't want your pity."

"Then accept my empathy. I can certainly relate to how you felt watching me with another man. But you know that already, don't you?"

At a sharp pain in his forefinger, he relaxed his grip on the rhinestone clasp of her purse. "I do?"

"Let's not insult each other by pretending ignorance, okay? You've developed some unsisterly feelings toward me in recent weeks. Tonight has been unpleasant for you, and I'm sorry I caused you pain. But…you were right about our kiss, and the way I feel about you.''

Everything in him grew still.

''I do want you—no! Stop!''

He pulled up short.

Her upraised palm came down. ''Please let me finish. I need to tell you a few things, before this—whatever *this* is—goes any further.''

He settled into a rigid stance about eight feet away.

She lowered her arm. ''I can empathize with how you felt watching me with Larry, because I've watched you flirt with every eligible woman in your vicinity except me in the past ten years. The difference is, I love you. I have since high school.''

His pulse stopped, then shot off the charts.

''I kept hoping that our professional relationship would become personal one day. In the meantime, you dated new women constantly, and I pictured each one touching you…and I wanted to…to hit something, or to, I don't know…''

''Howl?'' he supplied sickly.

''Yes!''

The fierce cry sliced away his last conceit. He'd put her through years of worse torment than he'd suffered tonight. He wasn't close to being worthy of that kind of devotion. Fear joined his other roiling emotions.

"Lizzy…" Half of him wanted to hold her tight and never let go; the other half wanted to get as far away as possible.

"You really didn't know, did you?" She'd regained her composure, and spoke with quiet dignity.

Her honesty deserved no less from him. "That you loved me? No. I was pretty sure you had a crush on me. That word sounds so juvenile, but you know what I mean. I thought that might be one reason why you were so loyal to the company, and I didn't want to rock the boat. I swear, though, I never meant to hurt you."

"I take full responsibility, Cameron. Don't feel guilty. For the most part, I've led a happy and productive life. As for my relationship with you…I preferred to dream about possibilities, rather than tell you how I felt. I was playing not to lose. I didn't want to risk finding out for sure that you'd never see me as more than a friend. But…"

In the space of a heartbeat, the tension between them subtly shifted.

"I don't play that game anymore," she continued in a low throaty voice.

His dormant arousal awakened instantly, even as his mind warned him of danger.

"You've changed," Cameron stated, struggling to focus his attention on her words.

"How?"

The night breeze stirred. A dark curl blew across her pale cheek.

He caught a whiff of her exotic scent, and his nostrils flared. "Your perfume is different," he said inanely. "You usually wear Lemon Spritz body cologne."

"I usually wear a lot of things I'm not wearing tonight."

Blood slammed from his brain to a more needy organ.

"I bought this dress to get your attention," she admitted. A graceful hand fluttered up to land delicately on her opposite shoulder. She adjusted a useless spaghetti strap. "If it didn't…"

He stared at the fingertips trailing from shoulder…to cleavage…to bodice, then flattening to stroke down her stomach. The disembodied illusion was intensely erotic.

"Well—" she gave invisible black satin and netting a swish "—I spent way too much money."

In the velvet night, she was as alluring and sensual as the perfume curling a come-hither finger beneath his nose.

"Li-zee," he warned in a voice he hardly recognized. "You're playing a dangerous game. And the prize you're hoping to win isn't a fling. You want a soul mate. A good man to share your life, and give you lots of babies, and love you as long as you both shall live." He sensed her taut attention. "I wish I could get down on one knee and say what you want to hear. God knows, I'm tempted. I care about you more than any woman I've ever known."

"But?"

"But I won't make a pledge I'm not sure I could keep in the future!"

"Did I ask you to? You're supposed to be a swinging eligible bachelor. Did you feel the need to propose marriage to all the other women you've slept with in the past?"

Jeez. "Other women didn't tell me they loved me. I'm trying real hard to be honorable, here, Lizzy."

"I know. And it's really getting on my nerves. I'm trying real hard to seduce you. Only it's not working. So I guess that means you're more honorable than I am sexy."

His heartbeat threatened to crack his ribs. He burned from the inside out. His entire body felt like one huge overstretched erection, hot and ready to burst. "I wouldn't say that."

"You wouldn't?"

He hoped like hell she knew what she was doing. "No."

"Then, for God's sake, Cameron, forget about the future! Stay with me tonight. It's my turn."

His control broke.

He closed the gap between them in three swift

steps and reached for her wrist. If he touched any more of her, they'd never make it inside the house.

"Not here," he said in a strangled voice. "Follow me."

WRIST CLAMPED in a bruising grip, Elizabeth stumbled when one of her three-inch-high heels wedged deep in a driveway crack. Cameron hauled her upright with a single one-armed heave. His strength was thrilling…and a little frightening. She bent to dislodge her shoe.

"Leave it," he ordered, towing her behind him with masterful strides.

She was forced to hobble after him Long John Silver-style or dislocate her shoulder. They moved from cement onto grass. Three steps later, her left heel drilled for oil. She managed to pull her foot free before he literally dragged her out of the shoe—but it was a close call. He never glanced back.

On the porch, she had a second's reprieve while he paused to open the door.

His face was expressionless. Hard and implacable. He looked like a man driven over the edge of his limits. And she was responsible!

Passive and electrified, she watched as he turned the knob and rammed his shoulder into wood. The door flew open and crashed against the wall. He surged inside, pulled her over the threshold, slammed the rebounding door and, only then, scooped her up in his arms as a groom carries his bride.

Her bittersweet pang was insignificant compared to the intoxicating ride across the den. She'd made this decision. A consenting adult aware of the facts. His emotions were tangled inseparably with his libido. He hadn't had years to sort them out.

But she had. And she wanted to express them at least once in the most intimate way possible, regardless of the outcome. If he never gave her his love in return, she would have memories of his desire as consolation. It was more than she'd ever thought to have.

Cradled in his strong arms, one hand feathering his hair, the other toying with a shirt stud, she felt feminine and weak. Wanton and powerful.

Am I dreaming? she wondered. *Is his fevered urgency really for me?*

He entered the hallway, grazing one of her stocking clad feet against the wall.

She curled closer, slipped her hand beneath the placket of his starched shirt, and marveled at his thundering heart. His chest was firm, the hairs silken. The tiny hard nub of his nipple tickled her palm.

Sucking in a breath, he quickened his pace. He reached the partially opened door of her bedroom and kicked his way through.

A small lamp on her chest of drawers provided a dim glow of light. He headed straight for the neatly made double bed. Her grandmother's bed, originally. The four-poster had comforted Elizabeth through chicken pox and pimples and unfulfilled girlhood dreams. She'd reclaimed her inheritance when she'd bought this house.

And her dreams had remained unfulfilled.

Suspended above her ivory comforter, Elizabeth gloried in the flesh and blood arms supporting her weight.

Then she was lying on a cloud of soft ticking, staring up at the face of a fallen angel, flawed and blessedly mortal. Beneath his self-centered drive to succeed beat the heart of a good man terrified of failing. In some areas of his life, anyway.

The eyes burning into hers with fearless intensity said his sexual prowess wasn't one of them.

As he stood motionless, his gaze moving over her slowly, a nervous flutter marred her anticipation. He'd dated so many beautiful women. He couldn't help but make comparisons.

"I can't believe this." His gruff voice sounded shaken. Bewildered. "I feel like it's my first time. I want you so much—" his ravenous gaze met hers "—I'm afraid to touch you."

Nothing could've disarmed her more effectively. She lifted and opened her arms. "Then let me touch you."

His eyes flared.

He ripped off his black jacket and flung it aside. His bow tie and cummerbund met the same fate. Enthralled, she watched the studs of his pleated shirt pop to land willy-nilly wherever they might. He tossed his cuff links on her nightstand, shrugged out of his shirt and pitched it atop the unlit lampshade. She had one tantalizing glimpse of lean torso before he dived into her welcoming arms.

Their mouths met with carnal familiarity, open and hot. Their tongues were voracious, their appetite fierce. They began at the heated stage where their last kiss had broken off.

Within seconds, Elizabeth was clawing at his smooth muscular back. His knee came up hard between her legs, and she writhed against the added stimulus of black netting. Moaning, she reached down to learn the shape and feel of him, to give him the same pleasured agony he delivered with his knee.

Her fisted strokes unleashed a ferocious ardor in his kiss she might've feared, had she not been just as wild for him. She tasted blood but didn't know whose and didn't care. Gentleness wasn't what she wanted. Wasn't what she needed. She was frantic to know all of him at once, lest she wake from her dream too soon.

He tore his mouth away to trail hot nibbling kisses from her neck, to her shoulder, to the swells above her bodice. More exciting than his kisses were the words he rained against her skin. He praised her beauty, he encouraged her boldness, he told her how she made him feel and what he wanted her to do to him. He described what he wanted to do to her in erotic language that planted arousing images. Her fertile imagination absorbed the words thirstily. Her passion unfurled like a lush tropical bloom.

At one point she was sitting up. When she lay back, her bodice flopped stiffly over her thighs. He divested her of both the dress and slip in one peeling motion, exposing her garter belt attached to black stockings.

The panties she'd bought to match were still in the sack.

"Je-e-eez," he said in a pained tone. "You're killin' me, here." He quickly straddled her knees.

She took in the muscular shoulders and arms that had carried her so effortlessly, the corrugated stomach his clothing normally hid. Flat copper nipples nestled within a sexy dusting of hair, darker than that on his head, and as soft as Lucy's ear, Elizabeth knew. Flattening her palms on his magnificent chest, she followed the silken arrow leading to his waistband. Her fingers fumbled to unfasten his pants.

He snatched both of her wrists with one hand.

She looked up into a furnace blast of smelted gold.

His nostrils distended. "You touch me, honey, and I'm gone. Besides—" he raised her limp arms above her head "—I wasn't finished touching you." He bent over and drew her nipple strongly into his mouth.

Her protest became a gasp.

The heat was stunning, his lips, teeth and tongue magical. She grew lost in a sensual fog of pleasure. The incoherent sounds coming from her throat seemed to fuel his efforts and passion to higher levels. He lavished her other breast with equal attention, then showered a lusty soliloquy down her quivering stomach. By the time he parted her thighs, she was melted butter. Her muscles couldn't have resisted if she'd tried.

The first touch of his most intimate kiss yet widened her eyes, then rolled them back in her head.

Her imagination had failed dismally to capture the exquisite sensations his ministrations produced. Embarrassment failed to take root in the environment he'd cultivated.

The climax rolled upon her like a thunderhead. First its shadow, then spattering droplets, then increasingly thick rain drumming without cessation. She thrashed her head, grabbed fistfuls of comforter, and cried out as lightning speared her once—twice. Grazed her lightly a third time and skittered away.

Oh, my.

Her arched spine eased down.

Oh, wow.

She melted into the mattress and opened slumberous eyes.

Cameron slid up beside her and lay on his side, elbow propped, head in hand. His eyes glowed with deep satisfaction, unslaked desire and a tenderness that swelled her heart.

"All better now?" he asked huskily.

"Much. But I do hurt a little."

Concern dimmed the heat in his eyes. "Was I too rough?"

She reached languidly to brush her knuckles against his zipper, stoking the furnace. "No. I'm aching to feel you inside me." She turned her hand and squeezed once, then let go. "Now get naked, before I have to slap you around."

"Promises, promises," he said, but wasted no time complying with her request.

He stripped off his remaining clothes in seconds flat, then pulled a condom from his pocket and ripped open the packet. His hands shook, and he swore softly. Elizabeth sat up to give him some help. She was very thorough, smoothing out every wrinkle—sometimes over and over—enjoying her task immensely. By the time she declared the job finished, Cameron's breathing was labored.

"Thanks," he said, pushing her gently, but firmly, back down. "I think I can manage from here on out."

At the first press of his naked body atop hers, Elizabeth released a shuddering sigh. Feeling his weight and hair-roughened skin, knowing her heart pounded against his, provided an element of closeness missing from her earlier pleasure.

He nudged her knees apart and crooned, "Lizzy, Lizzy. Why did we wait so long to do this?"

"Because you couldn't see what was right under your nose, you fool."

They were both smiling as he began the slow delicious slide forward. It had been a long time for her. She was tight, but more than receptive. Their moans mingled. Faded.

She stared solemnly at his beautiful face, awed by a sense of completion that had nothing to do with physical gratification, and everything to do with emotional contentment. Her heart expanded, swelled to bursting and could not be contained.

"I love you, Cameron." Reading a host of conflicting emotions in his blazing eyes, she pressed two fingers against his lips. "Shh. It's okay."

But suddenly it wasn't.

He kissed her fingertips fiercely and began the dance. A slow rhythm. Fluid and strong. Easing her ache to be as close to this man as nature made possible. Filling her heart with bittersweet joy that she experienced such love alone.

His beat accelerated, and the body she'd thought sated reawakened hungrier than ever, feeding on his growing passion. His earthy growls, his bared teeth, his rasping breaths, his corded neck. He hung his head to watch their bodies mesh, and her gaze followed. That was Cameron taking what she offered, giving her back unparalleled pleasure…and surely a portion of his love? The miracle of it burned hotter and hotter.

She welcomed every powerful thrust, lifted to receive him ever deeper. Her inner contractions shimmered in warning, then exploded, tearing a glad cry from her throat. She clung to his shoulders while he sought his own completion in a series of thrusts that skidded her along the mattress. He suddenly tensed, buried his face in her neck and let out a long masculine groan.

Their heartbeats gradually slowed.

Beneath his collapsed weight, she felt the rumble of his chuckle as if it came from her own chest.

What's so funny?'' she asked, hardly able to breathe, but not wanting him to move.

His chuckles increased.

She playfully punched his back. ''What is it?''

''I've gotta be the luckiest man alive.''

She smiled, unable to suppress her leap of hope.

Lifting up on his elbows, he smoothed back a curl sticking to her damp cheek. "First the agency picks up a slew of awards, then I beat out Sanderson for the most amazing woman in the world. Winning the SkyHawk account will make it a grand slam!"

He dropped a quick kiss on the frown between her eyebrows. "I haven't felt this good about the future in years! Thank you, Lizzy."

Fortunately, he didn't seem to expect an answer, since she couldn't speak past the terrible lump of regret in her throat.

CHAPTER THIRTEEN

LYING ON HIS SIDE, burrowed in softness, Cameron drifted awake slowly. A distant part of his mind warned him to cling to his tranquilized state. His body was warm and relaxed. Completely free of the tension that had never quite left him in recent months.

Why was that? he wondered groggily.

He opened his eyes to squint in the morning sunlight. Full consciousness hit him. No dark-eyed temptress sprawled with naked abandon beside him on the bed.

His bed.

Damn, but he wished he'd stayed asleep!

Flopping over onto his back, he flung a forearm over his eyes. By all rights he should be reaching out to spoon Lizzy's body close to his. He should be nuzzling her sensitive neck, smelling her herbal shampoo, filling his palms with her pretty breasts...

Ah, jeez, now he was more tense than ever.

Memories from the night before flashed behind his closed lids. Incredible didn't begin to describe her responsiveness, or his powerful reaction. Nothing in all his life compared with feeling Lizzy around him and under him as she stared up with love in her eyes. His mind-blowing physical climax hadn't ended the unique experience.

His emotional high had been equally explosive. He'd felt invincible. Able to conquer any challenge the future held, as long as he held her in his arms.

Most extraordinary of all, when he'd cuddled her close afterward, he hadn't counted the moments until he could leave without hurting her feelings, as he had with past partners. He'd felt humbled and blessed, tender and protective. He'd felt…contented, and he'd wanted to wake up beside her the next morning—a first for him.

Yet within an hour, she'd tucked Kara's purse beneath his arm and hustled him gently out of the house.

Last night, he'd chalked it up to post-intimacy shyness, and told himself they both needed space. A chance to adjust to their altered relationship.

Now…after his first decent sleep in weeks, and without her presence to fuzz his thinking, he wasn't so sure. Uneasiness gripped him.

Cameron lowered his arm, threw back the covers and swung his feet to the hardwood floor. He hadn't shown Lizzy his bedroom loft the night he'd served her dinner. She would've admired the fine craftsmanship of the pine armoire and matching king-size bed. He turned his head, and pictured her trailing appreciative fingers over the intricately carved headboard...then over his appreciative body—

He scrubbed his face with both palms. Maybe an omelette and the Sunday newspaper would distract him from other cravings.

After a quick shower and shave in the adjoining bathroom, he pulled on gym shorts and a gray T-shirt, then wound his way down the spiral staircase.

The soles of large bare feet, heels propped on the arm of his sofa, faced him as he headed for the kitchen. One foot bobbed a greeting, then slipped under a jumbled blanket along with its mate.

Jake sat up, laced his fingers beneath his dark whiskered chin and batted ridiculously long eyelashes. "Morning, darling," he said in a falsetto coo. "Sleep well?"

Answering with an appropriate hand gesture, Cameron entered the kitchen and started a pot of coffee brewing. His brother had been comatose on the sofa when he'd returned home last night. Jake was the only family member who'd accepted an invitation to stay at the condo instead of a hotel. He was always strapped for cash.

"Thanks for taking Carol home," Cameron said over his shoulder. "Sorry to dump her on you like that. She give you any trouble?"

"She gave me her phone number. She would've given me more than that, if I'd been half interested.

Man, with girlfriends like that, who needs enemies?''

Cameron was only beginning to comprehend what he'd been missing in life. ''She's not my girlfriend. That was our last date, I assure you.''

''Glad to hear it, bro.'' Silence. Then, ''You get Elizabeth's purse to her all right?''

Cameron turned and met innocent brown eyes. Too innocent for the brother he knew. ''Make yourself useful and get the newspaper outside the door. But first—what do you want to go with your omelette? Bacon, or sausage?''

Jake's smile lit the room. ''All ri-i-ight! I'll take bacon. And hey, no matter what Seth or Travis say I told them, you're my favorite brother.''

Cameron snorted, his mouth twitching. The youngest Malloy seemed happy to drift aimlessly through life, working for their father's sporting goods store, interested only in having a good time. He was slow to anger and quick to smile, an incorrigible jokester, and often, a huge pain in the ass.

But, like all the Malloy men, he would cut off his arm for Cameron should it be necessary, and vice versa.

Seconds later, Jake tossed a rolled newspaper on the island's black granite countertop. ''Do I have time to grab a shower?''

''A fast one. Use my bathroom. Fold the blankets

before you leave and take 'em up with you. They go in the bottom drawer of the armoire. Your wet towel goes in the hamper.'' Cameron turned around, opened the cabinet containing his omelette pan, and paused. ''Track water onto the hardwood floor, and you die,'' he yelled in afterthought.

''Yes, dear,'' came the falsetto response.

While Cameron pulled out ingredients from the refrigerator, he kept one ear cocked. The moment he heard the upstairs bathroom door close, he moved to a sleek red phone perched on the island.

Unbelievable! His hands hadn't shaken while dialing a ''girlfriend's'' phone number since he was a freshman in high school. His nervousness escalated with each progressive ring in his ear.

She picked up in the middle of the fourth. ''Hello?''

His heart floated. For the life of him, he couldn't suppress his big goofy grin. ''Hi, beautiful. You sound sleepy.''

''Cameron?''

He liked the breathless way she said his name. ''Did I wake you?''

''No…well, yes. What time is it?'' There was a fumbling noise. ''It's only eight o'clock. Is everything okay?''

Good question. But he should've waited another hour to find out. ''Yeah. Sorry to call so early, but I wanted to catch you before you made plans.'' He should've asked her last night. "Listen, Dad mentioned yesterday that Nancy wanted to buy a souvenir for Jeremy—that's her son. Actually, their son, but Dad isn't the blood father. Not that it matters. I just didn't know if you remembered who he is." Unbelievable. He was babbling!

"Of course I remember. How could I forget the strongest pitching arm in the nine- and ten-year-old division of Lake Kimberly's Little League?"

He blinked. "How'd you know that?"

"John bragged about it for ten minutes last night. He was so cute. Weren't you listening?"

Cameron had been too preoccupied watching Sanderson maul her across the table. "I've heard it so much I must've tuned him out. Anyway, I thought I'd take them shopping on The Drag before they leave Austin. The UT Co-op has tons of cool stuff a kid would like. I wondered if you'd like to join us?"

This was worse than sitting in a roller coaster, nearing the top of that first steep incline. "We'll probably have lunch somewhere on Sixth Street," he said, adding weight to his offer.

"O-oh, gee."

His stomach plunged. He'd used that tone too often himself not to recognize the sound of a brain being racked for excuses.

"That sounds nice. But I promised Mom I'd help her clean out her garage today. I'm sorry."

"Sure. No big deal." He could be wrong. After last night, giving him the brush-off made no sense. Taking a deep breath, he began the steep climb once again. "How about dinner tonight?"

"Dinner?"

God, he hated heights. "Yeah. I'd like to take you out to dinner tonight. On a date." There. Clear-cut and unmistakable.

"O-oh, I'm sorry. Mom's expecting me to stay for dinner. She's making pot roast."

Still, he hovered on the brink.

"Thanks for asking, Cameron, but I can't disappoint her. You understand."

He got the message loud and clear—and plunged faster and lower than before.

"Yeah, I know she's going through a hard time. Give her my best." He was proud of his credibly normal tone. "Guess I'll see you tomorrow at the office. Bye, Lizzy."

"Bye."

Her barely audible whisper sounded sufficiently distressed for him to ascend a few feet…

The dial tone flattened his hope.

He replaced the receiver carefully, and set about cooking breakfast with robotic dispassion. He'd just slid the second omelette onto a plate garnished with sliced tomatoes and cottage cheese, when Jake climbed down the steep staircase.

Reaching the ground floor, he heaved a loud sigh.

"How in hell do you keep from breaking your neck on those stairs after you've had a few drinks?" he asked, approaching the kitchen.

"I sleep on the sofa."

"Oh. Good thinking."

Jake had washed his hair, but hadn't bothered with a comb or razor. He wore threadbare jeans and a wrinkled Bass Busters Fishing Camp T-shirt. Malloy Marketing had designed the colorful screen print for Travis's business, and Malloy Sporting Goods Store sold the shirts to locals and tourists alike.

All for one, and one for all in his family. Though so far, Cameron had never asked for help.

Without being nagged, Jake gathered silverware, glasses and paper towels, then set two informal places at the island counter. Cameron poured orange juice, and they both sat.

His brother dug in enthusiastically, praising the meal, casting occasional glances his way.

Cameron's mushroom and cheese omelette tasted like sawdust. Halfway through, he gave up and laid down his fork.

Catching dark eyes studying him curiously, he shrugged. "I'm not very hungry. You want the rest of this?"

Jake drained the last of his juice before answering. "Nope. I want you to tell me what happened while I was in the shower."

Cameron hid his surprise. "I cooked you a breakfast fit for a king."

"When I left, you were bitching like normal. When I came back, you didn't say a word about my messy hair, or wrinkled clothes, or the paper towels I used as napkins. A second ago, I purposely put cottage cheese, tomato and a big bite of omelette on my fork."

"So?"

"Please. You hate it when I mix food on my fork. When we all lived at home, you used to carry your plate off in a huff and eat in the den, so you didn't have to look at me. But you watched me chew that bite just now, and didn't bat an eyelash. Something happened."

Despite teasing Cameron about his effect on the opposite sex, his brothers had come to him as the resident "expert" for advice about women. It was weird being the one to need advice.

Jake took the matter into his own hands. "It's about Elizabeth, right? She loves you. You love her. But something's gone wrong."

Cameron gaped.

"I'd like to claim brilliance, but after watching you growl at poor ol' Larry like he'd stolen your soup bone, we all figured it out. You're not worthy, but we want Elizabeth in the family too much to clue her in."

His family approved of Lizzy becoming a Malloy? Instead of irritation, he experienced a surge of pleased warmth.

"So what happened?" Jake persisted. "Did you call her while I was in the shower?"

Jeez. "You're a regular psychic hotline. Yeah, I did call her, as a matter of fact. I invited her to go souvenir shopping with me, Dad and Nancy. She said no."

"Smart lady."

"Then, I asked her to dinner tonight. I used the word 'date,' so she'd know that after ten years, I'm ready for the personal relationship she indicated last night that she wanted. She turned me down, again."

Brown eyes flickered, then steadied. "I'm sure she had a good excuse."

"She's eating pot roast with her Mom, whom I happen to know would be more than happy to share her pot roast. Only I wasn't invited."

Jake looked thoughtful. "So the phone call isn't the problem, but the symptom. I wondered why you came home last night. Did the deed not live up to her expectations, maybe?"

"What?"

"What d'ya mean, what? The great Casanova can't disappoint a woman like the rest of us schmucks? From the state of your clothes last night when you came in, it's obvious you did more than hand her a purse."

"I thought you were asleep."

"You thought I was asleep the night you met Mary Beth Hamilton on the football practice field, too. Doesn't mean I was."

"You followed me that night?" At age fifteen, Cameron had been more than eager to practice his passes with the seventeen-year-old cheerleader. His face heated. "You little pervert!"

"All thirteen-year-old boys are perverts. Gimme a break. Like you never spied on anyone at that age."

No. He'd waited until he was thirty-two. Cameron dropped the subject.

Jake forged on. "Elizabeth doesn't strike me as real...experienced. I mean that in a good way. Did you come on too strong and intimidate her?"

Cameron thought of the fingernail tracks he'd noticed on his shoulders while shaving. "No."

"Were you not forceful enough? God knows, walking that fine line between brute and wimp in a woman's mind is tough."

He remembered the high heels he'd forced her to abandon in his haste to get inside the house—and in her. "I wasn't a wimp. Look, I know for a fact she wasn't disappointed, okay?"

"Okay. Don't get offended." Jake broke off a piece of bacon and popped it in his mouth. "Did you roll over and fall asleep?"

"No."

"Did you get up and leave without cuddling first?"

"No!"

"Well, damn, bro. I'm stumped. What did she say after you told her you love her?"

Cameron opened and closed his mouth. He remembered the words knocking the back of his teeth to get out, and the huge effort it had taken to hold them back.

"Oh, man." Jake grimaced in disbelief. "Say it ain't so."

"Hey! I've never said the 'L' word to any woman before, and I won't, until I'm damn sure that what I feel will last, and I know our marriage would be a success. I was fair. She knew before anything happened last night that I couldn't make promises. She's okay with that."

"Bullshit! I was watching her at the ADDY Awards. She looked at you the way Nancy and Kara look at Dad and Travis. Elizabeth gave you her heart and soul long ago. Last night, she made love, whether you did or not. You got everything she has to give...and she got 'I'm not sure. I'll let you know later'?"

"That's not what I said!"

"Okay. What did you say? Exactly."

"Jeez, I don't know. You're the goddamn psychic. You tell me." But he did know. His gloating words about beating out Sanderson and winning the grand slam replayed with sickening clarity in his mind. As did her definition of playing to win. *It has nothing to do with "beating" someone else. It means that when we want something—whatever our goal or dream is—we go for it with everything we've got. We push ourselves to the limit, with no fear for what we might lose.*

Expelling a disgusted breath, Jake thrust fingers through shaggy wet hair, leaving it messier than ever. "Well, whatever you're not telling me, she is not okay with it, no matter what she told you. Sounds to me like this morning, she's decided to cut her losses and pull back, before you hurt her even more."

Cameron stared at the congealing omelette on his plate, and came close to ridding his stomach of the first half.

"You don't have much experience coping with disappointment, do you?" Jake asked in a quiet voice.

Wrong, Cameron thought. He'd disappointed himself more times than he could count.

"I wouldn't take this setback too hard," Jake continued. "You've been successful at everything you've ever tried. I'm sure marriage won't be any different."

Cameron had always secretly enjoyed his lazy younger brother's mixture of envy and pride in his accomplishments. One more sin for which he needed to atone.

He looked up. ''Your confidence isn't justified.''

''Sure it is. You always get what you go after. If you're worried about last night, you might have to work harder than usual to convince Elizabeth you really do love her, but you'll win her back.''

''That's what I'm afraid of.''

Jake looked startled, then dismayed. ''You don't want to win her back?''

''Oh, I want her back, all right. It's the 'work harder than usual' part I'm afraid of.''

Jake shook his head. ''You lost me, bro.''

''Let me make it simple.'' Cameron smiled grimly. ''I win what I go after, because I only go after the things in life that come easily to me. Put a real challenge in my path, and I crater before the first step.''

''Yeah, right.''

''Yeah, right,'' Cameron repeated in an unequivocal tone.

''Give me one good example.''

There were so damn many. But one in particular had changed the course of his life and corroded his self-esteem ever since. ''The summer before college, when knee surgery knocked me out of the football season? The surgeon said I'd never be a hundred percent, and he was right.

''The next year, after preseason practice, I told

Dad that being on the team really zapped my time and strength, and that in the long run, I'd be better off focusing my energy on academics. He tried to convince me that being third or fourth string quarterback was no shame, but my mind was set. I gave up my scholarship.''

''Cameron, you were one of the top high school recruits in the country. Hell, I've never seen any quarterback drive a team down the field better than you. You could've gone straight into pro ball before the injury. Of course you would've hated sitting on the bench. That's no crime. The odds against earning back your starting position were sky high. You shouldn't feel bad for not making the cut.''

''I don't. I feel bad for not even trying.'' Cruel justice, that he should finally admit his greatest weakness by confessing to Jake, of all people. ''Rehabilitation was the most painful hell I've ever gone through. I put out just enough effort to get back into walking condition. By the first day of preseason practice, I could run plays, but not like before.

''I didn't show up for practice the next day, or any other day. That's what I do, Jake, in case you still don't get it. When I face something that will really be tough for me to win, I give up before even trying. And I'll always regret...'' Nostalgic yearning swamped him. God, how he'd loved playing football!

He cleared his throat. ''I'll always regret not trying. I'll always wonder what would've happened if I'd pushed myself to the limits, instead of been afraid to fail. There are a lot of 'what ifs' in my life. Sorry to burst your bubble.''

Knowing he'd see disillusionment in his brother's eyes any second, Cameron forced himself not to look away.

What he saw was increasingly warm compassion, and a trademark hint of humor.

''You're sorry?'' Jake flashed his irrepressible grin. ''I can't tell you how happy I am to know you're human. I was beginning to wonder, since you never seem to lose.''

The lump Cameron had cleared from his throat returned larger than ever. When he could safely speak, his tone was wry. ''Winning is easy. It's losing that takes guts.''

Jake's amusement vanished. ''Take it from a clown and veteran underachiever. If you haven't ever risked failure to get something, don't beat yourself up. It only means you haven't come across anything—so far—that you're willing to push yourself to the limits to get.

''I'm no psychic, but you and Elizabeth have worked together ten years without splitting up. There's a camaraderie and mutual respect already there that usually takes years of marriage to build. The odds of success are in your favor right from the start.'' He ducked his head and sharpened his gaze. ''Am I right?''

''In theory, yes. But what if—''

''Let me make it simple. You loved playing football, and you could've found a way to stay close to the game, even if you couldn't play. But you chose a career in advertising, and you've lived just fine without football in your life. Am I right?''

''Yes.''

''Thank you. Okay, you love Elizabeth. Pretend for a minute that she's not in your life. Someone else sits in her office at the agency and attends staff meetings in her place. Someone else watches you pig out on Chuychangas and double dip chips in salsa. Someone else opens her arms to you in bed. Are you with me, here, bro?''

''Yes.'' And the images flashing in Cameron's mind sent a shudder through his soul.

''Okay, now we're getting somewhere! I'd say from your expression that the idea of living without Elizabeth is scarier than the idea of living with her and risking breaking up in the future. Am I right?''

''Yes.'' Instantly Cameron was filled with a sense of rightness, a conviction that Lizzy was the woman he wanted to grow old with.

Only she could fill his marketing VP's office, his booth at Chuy's Restaurant, and his bed with exactly the woman he needed, respected and loved. Only she made him want to become a better man.

"Yes," Cameron said louder. "You're right. Thanks for making it simple, Jake."

"Any time you need simple, I'm your man."

"Not hardly. Take it from a competitive over-achiever...anyone who writes you off as a clown or underachiever is a goddamn fool."

Jake's complexion turned ruddy. His Adam's apple slid up and down. And Cameron, for one of the few times in his life, looked into another person's eyes, and saw the reflection of a true winner.

CHAPTER FOURTEEN

"I DON'T UNDERSTAND," Elizabeth said, looking across her desk at Mitch, but intensely aware that Cameron watched her from the second guest chair. "On Friday, you agreed that eliminating the traditional 'first-class' section was a great idea. What changed your mind?"

Mitch frowned. "I'm not so sure we wouldn't be cutting off our nose to spite our face. I mean, SkyHawk has high-salaried executives to make those decisions. If we infringe on their territory in the presentation, they're going to feel threatened, and we won't get their vote."

Elizabeth drew a calming breath. Only two more hours, she counseled herself, and the Monday from hell would be over. She'd spent the day avoiding Cameron, explaining her swollen eyes to Rachel as privacy allowed and renewing various account team members' enthusiasm—when all she'd really wanted to do was curl up and cry. Mitch's conservatism, and his insistence that Cameron join their discussion, was an unexpected betrayal.

Fine. If the creative director wanted to think like a suit, she'd talk to him like one.

"Look at it this way. If Malloy Marketing gets the account, no way can we bill our considerable time and production costs invested in the spec presentation. We'll be adding staff in media, production and trafficking right off the bat. Cameron will have to exercise his lease option on the space next door. Overhead will go up at least a third, but efficiency depends on the learning curve of new employees. Just about the time the agency starts seeing a true profit, SkyHawk Airlines will either be a success…or not.

"If they crash and burn—" she eyed Mitch knowingly "—bye-bye to your cool big-budget TV commercials, ads in *Time* magazine and interviews with you in *Advertising Age.*"

He winced sheepishly, and she pressed her advantage. "If we got the account by catering to politics but our recommendations were faulty, then we truly would be cutting off our nose to spite our face. So it's in our best interest to help SkyHawk create the right passenger mix. Eliminating first class, for instance."

"Okay, okay. I'm convinced. Business and coach class, it is."

She glanced down at the latest results of her number crunching. "Actually…I think we should recommend another customer tier. A 'premium coach' class.''

"Hold on." Cameron interrupted at last.

As usual, meeting his eyes caused her stomach to flutter. "Yes?"

"I'm confused. I thought if we enticed the business flier, their fares would supplement the back of the plane."

"That's true. They would. But ideally SkyHawk shouldn't have to depend on business fliers to subsidize other passengers."

"And you're convinced another tier will increase profitability?"

"Their profitability, yes. They would set the actual prices, of course, but as long as 'premium coach' was cheaper than their business fare, and higher than competitors' economy fares, they couldn't lose. If we present a campaign based on sound revenue management principles, I can't imagine we'd step on any executive toes."

She braced herself before plunging on. "I've also reworked Susan's media budget, and funneled forty percent into public relations and airline service development. It means less money for Malloy Marketing initially...but, as I said, I think you'll forge a long-term partnering relationship that won't be easily broken."

His gaze intensified, holding hers captive. "A

long-term partnering relationship is definitely what I want.''

Now her heart fluttered along with her stomach.

''All right,'' he said abruptly, turning toward Mitch and allowing her to breathe again. ''We'll add 'premium coach' to our unique selling points in the launch campaign. You and Elizabeth work out the details. I trust you both implicitly.'' He scooted back his chair and stood. ''Now, if you'll excuse me, I have an appointment away from the office that I've put off far too long. I'll let Susan know about the budget reallocation before I leave.''

With a departing nod, he walked briskly out of the office.

Mitch and Elizabeth stared at each other in amazement.

He was the first to break the silence. ''Who was that masked man?''

''I don't know. But I'll bet you a dollar the real Cameron calls us from his car phone in ten minutes with more questions or instructions.''

Mitch linked his fingers loosely over his stomach. ''I've got kids to put through college. I can't afford to bet against the odds.''

As it turned out, he would have won this particular long shot.

She and Mitch spent the next uninterrupted hour brainstorming viable ''premium'' services that would offer perceived value to thrift-conscious travelers. Pete passed by her open door, and they waved him in to join the fray.

Over the weekend, he'd taken his notes from Friday's staff meeting and come up with a "Drive-Thru-Check-In" concept they all perfected now. A business-class passenger would board a SkyHawk Van from a satellite parking lot and hand the driver his ticket. The driver would radio ahead pertinent information so that when the passenger reached the airport, he'd be met at the van, handed a boarding pass and never lift a suitcase or stand in line.

It was exactly the kind of unique service that would allow SkyHawk to compete on the basis of quality, rather than price discounting. And from what Elizabeth knew of Gary Matthews, the unconventional ground service would appeal to the CEO's desire to offer a better total travel experience.

They decided to add it to their list of selling points.

When Pete glanced at his watch and cursed, she was shocked to look at her own wristwatch and see the time.

He jumped up and spoke on the move, "Sorry to bail, but the day-care center closes at six-thirty. They charge an extra ten bucks for every minute a parent is late." At the door, he gave a quick wave. "See y'all tomorrow."

"Ten bucks a minute," Mitch muttered incredulously. "We're in the wrong business."

"No kidding." She capped her pen and sank back into leather, signaling the meeting's end. Mental and physical exhaustion welded her body to the chair.

The creative director rose, arched his chest in a joint-popping stretch, then relaxed into his normal stoop-shouldered stance. He'd spent the first half of his career hunched over an art table. As technology and promotions had changed his job duties, he'd merely substituted a computer keyboard for an X-Acto knife. Elizabeth suspected that after twenty-five years, he wasn't capable of straightening his shoulders.

He met her eyes and smiled, etching deep lines in his skin and taking years off his age. "We got a lot accomplished, Elizabeth. I feel good about the direction we're going. You were right."

"Thanks, Mitch. The pieces are starting to come together. We'll get with the rest of the team tomorrow and fill them in."

"Sounds good." He scratched his beard. "You ready to leave now? I'll walk out with you."

"No. You go on. I want to straighten my desk before tomorrow."

"Okay. Don't stay too late." He was almost through the door when his hand shot out and clutched the jamb. He looked back over his shoulder. "I don't know about you, but I enjoyed the hell out of being 'trusted implicitly' to do my job, for once. Think it was a fluke?"

Lately, she hadn't been able to trust her instincts where Cameron was concerned. "I have no idea," she said honestly. "But I think we should take the ball and run with it from here on out. And while we're at it, we need to make darn sure Cameron doesn't have cause to regret his trust."

Mitch nodded thoughtfully, slapped the doorjamb once and then disappeared.

Elizabeth gazed bleakly at the empty doorway. The melancholy she'd held at bay for hours pressed her deeper into the chair.

Trust.

Such a simple word, to be so incredibly important in human relationships. Trust between parents and children. Employers and employees. Trust between friends. And lovers.

Especially lovers.

She closed her eyes, giving way at last to thoughts of the previous forty-eight hours. In all the years she'd fantasized about making love with Cameron, her imagination had never come close to the reality. Her lonely heart had seemed to burst free of her earthly form, then float back down, the emptiness filled.

She'd had mere moments to savor her rich contentment. Their bodies had not even separated before Elizabeth realized she'd already lost him.

Cruel justice, she supposed. She'd been so naive. Otherwise his exultant talk of winning wouldn't have dealt a fatal blow to her heart.

After all, she'd deliberately exploited his competitive nature. He'd noticed her, pursued her and bedded her just as she'd dreamed—no, just as she'd schemed. She should've been blissfully happy. Phase one of her marketing plan was a complete success.

In phase two, according to her goals and objectives, his fear of commitment would vanish and they would build a future together. She would be everything Cameron wanted and needed. They would live happily ever after. The end.

Never once while dreaming and scheming had she considered what she wanted and needed from him.

And she wanted all he had to give—not whatever portion he could spare from other interests, ambitions or responsibilities. She needed him to be the one constant in life that she could count on, for richer or for poorer, for better or for worse. What she wanted, what she *needed* before sharing a life with him, was to be able to trust in his love.

Thanks to her own "brilliant" plan, she had, indeed, cut off her nose to spite her face.

A long-term relationship is definitely what I

want, he'd said only hours ago, despite being turned down for a date the day before. The look in his eyes had seemed to support his words.

But he'd had ten years to say those words, and he hadn't. Ten years to show any romantic interest at all, and he hadn't. Not until she'd manipulated and plotted and made herself a prize to be won had he said them. How could she trust any future avowal of love he might make?

The heartbreaking answer was she couldn't.

The sound of a vacuum cleaner in the hallway jerked her thoughts back to the present.

She opened her eyes, swiveled her chair and looked dully out her window. A pearl-white moon, unnaturally huge, rose sluggishly on the horizon. Beyond the twinkle of downtown lights, the UT "Tower" glowed orange. The basketball team must've won their game earlier.

Cameron would be pleased.

Fighting the sting of tears, she turned back to her cluttered desk. The task of straightening out her paperwork was suddenly overwhelming. Getting herself home would take all her remaining stamina. She retrieved her purse from a bottom drawer and left her mess behind to tackle it in the morning.

When she almost tripped over the heavy-duty cord stretched across her doorway, the vacuum cleaner switched off.

"My fault, Tom," she said with a wave. "I'm

okay.'' She knew all the regular cleaning crew by name, since she worked late so often.

The grizzled man smiled and ducked his head. "You be careful drivin' home, now, hear?"

"I will, thanks. Good night." She hitched her shoulder strap and headed for the lobby, his kindness thickening her throat.

She was an emotional wreck. Since Cameron had left Saturday night, she'd cried at every little thing. Breaking a cereal bowl. Forgetting to give Lucy her heartworm pill. Sitting down to more pot roast than she and her mother could eat in three nights. Muriel had grown alarmed at the role reversal, and demanded to know what was wrong with her rocksteady daughter.

Elizabeth pushed through the glass lobby doors and punched the "down" elevator button.

She hadn't had the heart to complain about losing a love she'd never had, to a woman mourning the death of a thirty-five-year marriage.

Five minutes later she drove south on I-35 and revised her goals and objectives for the next two weeks. She would be out from under Cameron's nose after the presentation. But until then, she would have to continue today's charade and pretend that her heart wasn't breaking. When he asked her out again—and he would—she would politely refuse and explain that she...

That she what?

That she didn't love him? She couldn't pull off that deception. A hot tear rolled down her cheek.

Well, then, she would simply tell him they needed to slow down and evaluate the situation before proceeding. She would manufacture other commitments requiring her time. Eventually he would see her not as an irresistible challenge but an irritating nuisance not worth his trouble.

And if he didn't—

Oh, God, she couldn't let herself hope that he wouldn't give up his pursuit. From now on she would live each day firmly grounded in reality.

A second tear slipped from her blurry eyes.

She would halt the progress of their romantic relationship while she still had the strength to do so. Allowing it to build, knowing full well the foundation was weak, would only lead to greater pain. Her mother and father were proof of that.

By the time Elizabeth turned onto Jackrabbit Lane, she'd given up trying to stem her pathetic sniffles, and drove on automatic pilot. She longed for a cool cloth on her face, a glass of wine and her dog—not necessarily in that order.

The golden retriever was the one good thing to come from Elizabeth's scheming. Her one joy in the pit of misery she'd dug for herself. Lucy had belonged to a woman moving into a small New York City apartment. The owner's tremendous loss was Elizabeth's huge gain. After only six days, she couldn't imagine how she'd survived without that doggy grin and wagging tail welcoming her home, or the click of nails on pavement beside her during morning jogs through the neighborhood. Lucy was well mannered, housebroken, sweet tempered, and…well, *there*. She'd transferred her unconditional love to her new owner without a hitch, and wedged herself permanently into Elizabeth's heart.

Elizabeth realized she'd stopped crying the same instant she noticed where she was. Braking, she twisted around to look at the Jaguar parked in the driveway two houses back.

Cameron is here?

Her heart beat erratically.

Cameron is here!

Elizabeth turned back around, grabbed her purse, yanked out a tissue and scrubbed at her face. No makeup at all was better than telltale rivulets through powder and blush. Nothing she could do about her splotchy skin, though.

Cameron is here!

She shifted gears and drove carefully in reverse to park in front of her house. Not wanting to block his car, she parked at the curb. He wasn't in sight.

But, oh, his handiwork was.

She stared at the double spotlight installed above her garage under the eaves, the reason she'd driven past her own house. Her brightly lit front yard looked foreign to her stunned eyes.

Elizabeth locked her car and walked up the driveway in a daze, noting her drastically shortened but neatly trimmed cedar bush.

A sharp bark and a deep laugh steered her feet in a new direction. She unlatched the fence gate, slipped through and moved through the dark narrow space between wood fence and clapboard house. The backyard, lit only by the moon, loomed ahead.

Ferocious growls erupted, joined by rumbling chuckles. She rounded the corner of her house...and slowed to a stop.

Sitting in the grass beyond the small cement patio, knees up and sneaker treads digging for traction, arms stretched between his braced legs, Cameron clasped one end of a knotted rope toy. Lucy grasped the other with her bared teeth. Her crouched body trembled with strain, her eyes slitted in ecstasy, her paws hitched backward in fractions of an inch.

Tug-of-war was her favorite game in the universe. She would play it until Elizabeth's arms ached and she gave up in defeat.

But in Cameron, Lucy had finally found a worthy opponent. Both man and dog were engrossed in the battle.

And Elizabeth, for the first time all day, allowed herself to look her fill of the man.

Awash in moonlight, his tanned face was a swarthy contrast to hair shimmering a strange colorless hue. His bluish-white T-shirt undulated over broad shoulders; denim pulled taut over powerful thighs. Reflector patches on his shoes glowed neon green. Were his bare feet white? She couldn't remember, and her heart twisted. She'd probably never know.

Gazing at arms roped in muscle, she recalled the way he'd carried her effortlessly and made her feel intensely desirable...and desired. How, she wondered in anguish, had she ever thought the memory would be a consolation?

It would torture her the rest of her life.

As if pulled by her terrible yearning, his head turned and he met her stare. The lupine gleam of his eyes set off tiny shocks of awareness in her body.

Without smiling, he faced the dog again, and with one mighty pull, dragged Lucy between his knees and clamped her ribs tight. He worked the toy free of her teeth, threw it aside, grasped her ears in each hand, then spoke nose to muzzle in a cavern-deep voice.

"We'll have to call it a standoff, girl. Your master is finally home."

He opened his thighs. "Now, go say hello."

Lucy got in three good licks on his mouth before, sputtering, he gently but firmly pushed her back.

Elizabeth laughed. Apparently no female was immune to that gorgeous face.

With a joyful bark, the dog bounded toward Elizabeth. She lowered herself to her knees to receive her own sloppy kiss, ruffle silky fur and croon a stream of nonsense.

"Hello, pretty girl. Did you miss me today? I missed you. Are you hungry? Want to go in the house while I get your food?"

Fumbling inside her purse, she spun away from the cold nose vying for her hand's attention, then pulled out a jumble of metal. She separated the back door key from the others, clambered to her feet, turned around to take a step—and jerked back.

Strong hands clasped her upper arms, steadying her balance.

"Whoa, there. Didn't mean to scare you." Cameron's hands gentled, but remained put. "I only wanted to let you know the spotlight switch is inside the garage next to the side door. But it's on an automatic timer, set to go on at 6:30 p.m. and off at the same time every morning. You'll have to reset it as the days get shorter, okay?"

Staring up at his tender expression, she could not for the life of her muster the will to break his grip. "Okay."

"You look beat. That boss of yours is working you too hard."

Remembering her ravaged face, she regretted the full moon. "Mom's working me too hard," she said, not untruthfully. "She's a pack rat. It took her thirty years to accumulate a garage full of junk.

Boxes and boxes, some too heavy to lift, and she expected us to clear it out in one day. We didn't come close to finishing.''

''Sorry to hear that.''

She thought briefly that he sounded more relieved than sorry, but shrugged it off. ''Thank you for my spotlight. I can't believe you went to so much trouble. And the bush looks nice, too. Please let me know how much you spent, and I'll reimburse you.''

He frowned. ''I did it as much for my peace of mind as anything. I don't want your money.'' His eyes glittered.

Her heart beat wildly.

He tightened his hands.

Wide-eyed, she unconsciously parted her lips.

Releasing her arms, he stepped back and took the key ring from her limp fingers.

She watched him unlock her back door, push it open and wait. Lucy raced over and rushed into the house.

As if in a trance, Elizabeth walked toward him, scarcely able to breathe for her hammering heart. *He wants to come inside. Oh, God. Does he expect a repeat of Saturday night?*

She brushed past him, aware of his heat with every pore of her skin.

In the doorjamb, she turned around. ''Cameron...I don't—''

''G'night, Lizzy.'' He cut her short.

Extending the keys, he pressed them in her palm and folded her fingers closed. For a heart-stopping moment, his warm strong hand engulfed hers; his thumb rubbed the fluttering pulse at her wrist.

''Sweet dreams.'' He removed his hand.

White teeth glinted in the moonlight before he turned and sauntered toward the gate.

Elizabeth stared numbly at the glorious full moon until long after she'd heard the Jaguar drive off.

CHAPTER FIFTEEN

ELIZABETH WAS among the first to arrive at the office the next morning. Someone had already made two pots of coffee, thank goodness. After the restless night she'd spent, she needed a whole pot all to herself.

At about 3:00 a.m., after interpreting his actions forty different ways, she'd finally admitted to herself that she'd wanted Cameron to kiss her—or at least try to, anyway. She'd counted herself lucky that he hadn't, and then strengthened her resolve to resist the undeniable physical chemistry between them.

He'd done a kind deed, and she would leave it at that.

The fact that she'd slipped on a new dress this morning, bought along with the black satin one she'd worn to the ADDY Awards, was purely coincidental. And if her heart insisted on warming every time she thought of her floodlights, it was only because he'd spent hours that couldn't be billed back to clients, not because he'd needed "peace of mind."

She'd just added cream to her coffee when she caught a whiff of Obsession perfume.

Without turning, she filled a second foam cup and added a packet of sweetener. "Morning, Rachel."

"You should be a mother. Eyes in the back of your head is a terrible thing to waste."

Elizabeth picked up both cups, turned around and extended her right hand. "How is motherhood these days, by the way?"

A beatific smile lit Rachel's face as she accepted her coffee. Wearing a long navy shirtdress with side slits to above the knee, her waist cinched with a silver buckled belt, she looked slim, young and vibrant.

"Motherhood's great. It's like Ben's body was snatched and replaced with a new kid. I'm almost afraid I'll start noticing a bunch of pod people in the neighborhood."

Chuckling, Elizabeth waved her friend to follow and headed for the farthest of six round black laminated tables. The "coffee room" doubled as a lunchroom with full kitchenette and was about four times the size of her spacious office.

The agency wouldn't officially open for twenty minutes. They settled down to indulge in a chat.

Rachel's smile grew sly. "Is that a new dress?"

Taking a sip of coffee, Elizabeth mumbled against the rim, "Maybe."

"First angora. Now this. You're turning into quite the little sweater bunny, aren't you?"

Elizabeth looked down at the rib-knit lamb's wool. In the store, she'd thought the forest-green color seemed nice with her dark hair and eyes. But…was the turtleneck style too tight?

"Elizabeth, I'm teasing! You're a knockout. Has Cameron seen you yet?"

"I don't think he's come in. So…Ben has shaped up his act, you say?"

With a knowing look, Rachel allowed the subject change. "Since Steven moved back home, Ben and I haven't had one argument. He's been on his best behavior. Rabbi Levitz told me he's seen a huge improvement in Ben's Hebrew. I'm even beginning to think he won't humiliate himself this weekend in front of a synagogue full of people."

Elizabeth shook her head admiringly. "I can't believe he's leading the service. What a lot of pressure for a thirteen-year-old."

Panic flickered in Rachel's deep blue eyes.

Real smart, Elizabeth. "Don't worry. He'll do great."

"His self-confidence is only part of my worries." Rachel affected a shudder. "I have nightmares about Steven's mother being served a big fat juicy pork chop at the luncheon."

Elizabeth almost choked on her sip of coffee, then looked closer at her friend's expression. She sobered. "You've talked to the chef. You've got a contract with a written menu. Nothing will go wrong. You've thought of everything."

She'd been amazed at the amount of advance planning celebrating Ben's becoming a Bar Mitzvah involved.

Rachel and Steven would host the "Oneg Shabbat" refreshment break after Friday-evening services, a luncheon after Saturday-morning services and a dance party for Ben on Saturday night. And that didn't count the years of religious study Ben had had, which helped him to prepare for his big event!

Rachel had grown pale. "Did I tell you Steven's aunt Davinia is flying in from New York?"

Only about four times since last Wednesday morning, after Steven had called and informed his wife of the intimidating news.

"Quit giving her the power to terrorize you, Rachel. So what if her grandson had a filet mignon dinner for two hundred adults and a live band for the kids' party? You're not competing for most money spent."

"Tell that to Steven's mother." Rachel began systematically notching the rim of her foam cup with the edge of a glossy red thumbnail.

"If Aunt Davinia looks down her nose at the pecan-crust chicken or a disc jockey playing CDs—

then she's a snob and a bitch and who cares what she thinks?''

"Steven's mother."

"Oh, c'mon. Give her more credit than that. What she cares about is watching her grandson enter symbolic adulthood. What she cares about is seeing him affirm his commitment to lead a responsible Jewish life."

Rachel lifted her cup and sipped from a small nonmutilated portion of rim. "Hmm."

"You know I'm right."

"I suppose."

"There's no suppose about it."

"Hmm." The last bit of smooth foam bit the dust.

"Shoot, she'll be so proud of Ben, she won't even notice that big fat juicy pork chop on her plate."

Rachel's gaze jerked up, then narrowed.

Elizabeth laughed. "You'll think that's funny next week."

"If I don't have a nervous breakdown before then."

The sound of masculine laughter preceded three production artists, entry-level employees fresh out of college, walking in to pour themselves coffee. Elizabeth and Rachel smiled politely, then huddled closer together, backs to the room, leaving them to jostle each other, talk sports and be guys.

"Listen," Elizabeth said for Rachel's ears alone, "I'm glad to know that Ben's behaving these days. But what about you, little girl?"

"Huh?"

"Have you been naughty or nice since Steven's been home?"

Instantly a blush stained Rachel's cheeks.

"Ahh. Good for you." Elizabeth took a sip of coffee. "The first counseling session must've gone well."

Rachel reached out suddenly and clasped Elizabeth's free hand in both of hers. "The best thing that ever happened to me was you asking for my help with your love life. You made me not only confront Steven, but myself. We're going to be okay, Elizabeth. Better than okay. I feel almost like a new bride."

Obviously the foundation of her relationship with Steven had been strong enough to weather a rough storm.

Elizabeth ignored her twinge of envy. "I'm so glad."

More people wandered in for their morning cup of coffee, providing, oddly, more privacy than before.

Rachel's expression softened. "You look so tired, hon."

Oh, God, not the blasted tears again.

"I hate to see you this unhappy. Won't you reconsider your decision?"

"No." Elizabeth gently pulled her hand from her friend's compassionate clasp. "It's for the best. And I'm fine. I promise."

Though she'd confided everything up to this point, she preferred keeping last night to herself. No sense making Rachel question the wisdom of halting a "love life" she'd helped create.

"I'm fine," Elizabeth repeated to the warm concern in blue eyes. "You save your worry for the Bar Mitzvah."

"Okay, okay. I'll leave you alone." Rachel arched a brow. "But can we at least time our nervous breakdowns so we'll be at the funny farm together?"

They exchanged a look of amused affection, during which the atmosphere behind them subtly changed. Voices quieted.

The back of Elizabeth's neck prickled. She widened her eyes and silently mouthed, "Cameron."

Both women shifted to face the room.

A variety of greetings rang out from the seven loitering employees—everything from "Hi, Cameron," to "Good morning, Mr. Malloy," depending on age, sex, tenure with the company and/or self-confidence level.

Rachel cast an impressed glance at Elizabeth and muttered, "A terrible thing to waste."

But Elizabeth didn't need eyes in the back of her head to identify Cameron's presence. Her seismographic body had registered his vibrations instantly. Their gazes connected briefly, and she experienced the familiar earthquake in her chest.

His designer suit was charcoal gray, his tie a tasteful red-and-gray print. The bronzed face above his starched white collar was as handsome as ever, but he seemed…different, somehow.

He nodded hello to her and Rachel, then turned to pour his own coffee. As he smiled and answered a few questions regarding the upcoming presentation, she struggled to pinpoint the change.

Minutes later, realizing that the room had grown ever more crowded, she had her answer.

Normally an appearance of "the boss" sent employees scurrying to their desks, hanging up from personal phone calls, striving to look busy and productive so he wouldn't stop for an impromptu grilling. Woe unto the staff member who couldn't provide a satisfactory status report.

But this morning he was asking questions of a personal nature. Had Jarod played basketball in college? How early did Linda have to leave her house in Round Rock in order to make it to work on time—and Jeez, how could she stand that? Why had Don decided to grow a mustache?

Studying Cameron's relaxed friendly expression, Elizabeth saw that he wanted to learn the answers.

That was what had changed. The cool distance he usually maintained with all but the highest-level staff members was gone.

Watching each face he focused on light up, and the way employees crowded eagerly around him, as if he were a celebrity, she knew that each one of them felt special and flattered. His charisma had that effect on people. She was no exception.

No exception at all.

She turned and caught worried blue eyes studying her as carefully as she'd studied Cameron.

Elizabeth forced a smile. "It's almost eight. I'd better get to work."

"Me, too. The phones will start ringing any second," Rachel said ruefully.

They stood and tossed their cups into a nearby trash can. The sharpest employees in the room noted the time and followed suit. Several seized the opportunity to get even chummier with Cameron. Most notably a curvy young redhead from account services named Kim, aka "Kimbo the Bimbo" in uncharitable office gossip.

Tearing her gaze from the dainty hand clinging to his arm, Elizabeth moved with Rachel and the others toward the door.

"Want me to beat her up for you?" Rachel murmured. "I can take her, you know. She's younger— but I'm meaner."

Elizabeth smiled shakily at her dear friend, who

continued staring unabashedly at Cameron's entourage of brownnosers and brazen flirt.

About three yards from the door, Rachel purred, "Well, well. Looks like he just brushed Kimbo off." She stiffened, then pinched Elizabeth's arm. "Look alive."

"Lizzy, wait!"

Lizzy?

Flustered, Elizabeth turned to see Cameron covering the distance between them in long determined strides. He'd never used her nickname in public before, and she sensed the fascinated stares of everyone still inside the room. The purposeful gleam in his eyes made her nervous.

When he stopped so close she was forced to tilt up her face, she stepped back for more oxygen.

He followed.

Her pulse rate tripled. She managed a small "Yes?"

His gaze moved over lamb's wool, her mouth, then back to her eyes. The gleam in his had intensified. "You look extra nice today."

This was the third time she'd heard that phrase. But its impact only strengthened with repetition. "Th-thank you."

Painfully aware of his inappropriate nearness, and their captivated audience, she made it through five exploding heartbeats before blurting, "Did you want something?"

"Hmm? Oh. Just to say good morning."

Then, as casually as if he did so every morning, and they were completely alone, he dropped a soft brief kiss on her stunned mouth.

When his head came up, his eyes were smiling. "There's a SkyHawk account team meeting at one o'clock. Don't forget."

He walked past his gaping employees with a total lack of self-consciousness and disappeared through the door.

In the vaultlike silence, a single voice spoke for them all.

"Oy!"

FOR THE REST of the day, he didn't so much as glance at Elizabeth funny. Nor did he seek her out to say goodbye before she left, or race to beat her home—she'd searched up and down the street for a parked Jaguar, much to her self-disgust.

She played with Lucy, watched a little TV and jumped every time the phone rang.

No, she didn't want to switch long-distance companies. No, she didn't want a free estimate for vinyl siding. No, she didn't "happen to know" if her mother had sold the pool table and jukebox as threatened and put her sewing machine in the game room. Her father's thinly veiled efforts to pump her for information his lawyer could use were hurtful but familiar. She went to bed exhausted, disheartened and confused.

Why had Cameron kissed her in front of God, country and gossip-prone employees, yet not in the privacy of her moonlit backyard? Despite her unanswered questions, she slept hard and deep, and woke feeling surprisingly refreshed.

Her morning jog with Lucy cleared the last cobwebs from Elizabeth's mind. Cameron's agenda was still unclear, but forewarned was forearmed. If he pulled something like that again, she wouldn't stand there like Kimbo the Bimbo. No sirree, Elizabeth vowed. She would demand explanations and persist until she got them!

At five minutes before eight, dressed in a classically tailored taupe pantsuit at least three seasons old, she walked into the crowded coffee room at Malloy Marketing and stopped conversation cold. Then everyone started talking more loudly than before, and all at once.

Yep. She'd interrupted a gossipfest starring "Lizzy," all right. Disconcerting, to say the least. Especially the speculative glances of the men, and the skeptical reassessment of the women.

She fled to her office.

CAMERON SPENT most of the day away from the agency, visiting clients. No matter how competent the account executives were, they didn't have the clout, panache or perceived importance of the founding owner. A "How are we doing?" visit from him every couple of months caught discontent before it became defection. His responsiveness smoothed rough spots and solidified existing good relations.

He returned to the agency around three o'clock, and stopped by her office soon after.

For ten heart-pounding minutes she reviewed her latest ministudy. It would actually cost more for SkyHawk Airlines to recycle used Walkman-style padded headsets—one of the quality upgrades Malloy Marketing was recommending—than to give them away "free" to deplaning passengers. Why not seem innovative and exceptionally generous?

He was enthusiastic, complimentary and frustratingly impersonal. "Add it to the list," he said before leaving her office.

She didn't see him again that day.

That night she played with Lucy, watched a little TV and turned down a subscription to the local newspaper she already received, a preapproved "special introductory rate" major credit card and a free weekend to a resort complex on Lake Travis—if she attended a "brief" sales presentation Saturday morning from eight until noon. She no longer jumped when the phone rang.

Grumpy, tired and wondering why she'd blown such a little kiss all out of proportion, she crawled into bed at ten o'clock.

When the phone rang at ten-thirty, she bonked herself in the eye with the receiver, shifted it to her ear and mumbled, "'lo?"

Startled silence, then, "Elizabeth?"

She buried her face in her pillow and groaned.

"Elizabeth? Are you all right?"

Lids glued shut, she turned her head. "Yes, Mom. You woke me."

"Oh. You're usually such a night owl, I didn't think I'd disturb you. I'm sorry. I'll talk to you another time about Cameron."

Elizabeth's eyes popped open.

"Good night, honey."

She clambered onto her elbows. "What about Cameron?"

"I know you're tired. He said you'd been working too hard on that big airplane account. You go on back to sleep and we'll talk tomor—"

"Mom!" Every trace of grogginess had swept away on a flood of adrenaline. "When did you talk to Cameron?"

"Tonight." Her mother sounded puzzled. "Didn't you know he was coming to help clean my garage?"

"No-o."

"Well, goodness! He called yesterday and said you'd mentioned how heavy some of those boxes were, and he asked if tonight would be convenient for him to help me."

Elizabeth collapsed, then rolled over onto her back.

"Oh, honey, you'll never believe how much we got accomplished! He borrowed a truck from Mitch—I think that's who he said—and we filled... Well, he filled the back of the truck almost completely. He's very strong...." Her mother trailed off dreamily.

"Mo-ther!"

"What? I'm not allowed to notice? That is one gorgeous man you work for. And his heart is beautiful, too. My, how we talked and laughed. The hours flew by...."

Elizabeth didn't scold this time. Recalling how often she tuned out her mother's "trivial" chatter, she realized Muriel was starved for attentive company.

"Anyway, he drove straight from here to Madeline Wilson's. She just called, ecstatic over everything I donated to the Garden Club yard sale. It's sure to be a success now. And best of all, I can park my car in the garage!"

Despite good intentions, Elizabeth tuned out most of her mother's remaining conversation. At eleven o'clock, she hung up the phone, punched her pillow, snuggled down and pulled the comforter up to her chin.

Three hours later, her nightgown twisted around her thighs, her sheets a tangled mess, her comforter spilling off the bed, she finally drifted into sleep.

CHAPTER SIXTEEN

SITTING IN a packed synagogue, Cameron on one side of her, a contingent from Malloy Marketing on the other, Elizabeth cursed her lack of foresight.

She should've known Saturday morning's service would get to her, and prepared accordingly. Didn't she always cry at Hallmark moments? Plus, the emotional roller coaster she'd been on lately made her even more prone to loss of control. The measly single tissue she'd stuffed in her jacket pocket wasn't going to cut it. Stupid, stupid, stupid.

She'd dredged an emergency backup tissue from her purse, but it was stained with lipstick and slightly decomposed. Water would melt it faster than it would a Wicked Witch.

Oh, damn. There went another one.

Elizabeth carefully dabbed at the new tear sliding down her cheek.

She'd suspected she was doomed early on, when Steven's seventy-five-year-old father had presented Ben with a beautiful embroidered tallith. What a picture they'd made facing one another! The elderly gentleman, silver-haired and slightly stooped, with a lifetime of responsibilities, sorrows and joys behind him; the handsome teenager, straight and strong, only beginning his adult journey.

Melvin had draped the prayer shawl around his grandson's neck so lovingly, spoken of pride in an unbroken chain of tradition so eloquently, Elizabeth had been helpless to prevent the first tear from spilling free.

In her experience, that was the deciding tear. Hold it back, and chances for sustained composure were good.

Let it fall, and others pushed and shoved from behind to blubber free, dignity and makeup be damned.

On the platform, Rachel sat in a high-backed chair next to Steven, the rabbi and the cantor. All four faced the congregation, though Ben stood front and center behind the pulpit. Rachel's expression reflected the fierce love and pride, the hope for the best—and fear of the worst—that mothers since the beginning of time had felt for their sons. And watching her watch him…Elizabeth experienced some of those same emotions.

He looked so tall and mature, in his new blue suit with the pants that actually fit. He'd read aloud in Hebrew from his Torah portion without a stumble. He'd instructed the congregation in an authoritative, deeper voice than she remembered, telling them when to stand, sit, recite and turn pages.

Knowing of Rachel's battles to get him to study, Elizabeth was amazed and impressed at his competence and poise. Now he was ready to deliver the "speech" his mother had despaired of his ever writing, much less delivering with ease.

Elizabeth's stomach fluttered with empathetic nervousness.

"My Bar Mitzvah Torah portion focuses on Abraham, his son Isaac and a test from God," Ben began in a strong confident voice. "Back in Abraham's day and age, most people worshiped many different gods, and some religious cults practiced human sacrifice. So when God told Abraham to go to the land of Moriah and sacrifice Isaac as a burnt offering, the order probably didn't seem as horrible then as it does today."

Good, Elizabeth thought. His gaze continually scanned the congregation. He wasn't focused on one spot like a deer in the headlights.

"Still, Abraham loved his son very much. We can imagine his pain as he built an altar, laid out the wood, bound Isaac and laid him on top of the wood, then raised the knife to carry out God's will." He paused to let that sink in. "At the last second, an angel of the Lord called from heaven and stopped Abraham from killing his son, then told him to sacrifice a ram in place of Isaac."

Either he'd practiced more than Rachel realized, or he was a natural-born storyteller. Elizabeth glanced at the interested faces around her, and looked proudly back at Ben.

"One of the reasons Jews blow the shofar, or ram's horn, at Rosh Hashanah and at the end of Yom Kippur services is to remind us of two things Abraham learned from his test. The first is that the religion of his God is morally superior to the religion of heathen gods. The second reminder is that God values our obedience and trust above all else."

His manner shifted and became friendlier. Chattier.

"When I wrote this speech, I had an outline to follow. It said for me to tell why my Torah portion is as meaningful today as it was in ancient times." He made a very modern teenage face. "My mind was blank. So I asked my parents this question. If God asked you right now to sacrifice me as a burnt offering...would you do it? And they said..."

He paused dramatically.

"Can we get back to you on that when you're eighteen?"

While chuckles snowballed into laughter, he threw an affectionate glance over his shoulder at Steven and Rachel.

Elizabeth and Cameron exchanged matching grins. That was a Rachel comment if ever they'd heard one.

Ben's smile faded and he adopted a serious tone. "But then we talked about the role of moral beliefs and obedience in modern life, and what might happen in a world without them. What if, for example, Americans didn't believe in the moral rights and freedoms outlined in our constitution, and another country declared war on us and launched an attack? Our citizens wouldn't obey the draft call, like Abraham obeyed God.

"Parents wouldn't send their sons and daughters into battle to die, like Abraham was prepared to sacrifice Isaac. If no American believed in or obeyed a set of moral rules and customs, German would probably be our language today."

Like everyone else, Elizabeth recalled family members whose fate and histories were inextricably tied to a war. She shuddered at what many in the room must be remembering.

"There were times—" Ben shrugged and grinned, his braces endearing "—okay, a lot of times, in the past that I didn't think it was fair that I had to come home from regular school and turn right around and go to religious school. I wanted to play. But instead I obeyed my parents and studied Judaism's beliefs and customs. I even learned Hebrew well enough to lead services without messing up too many words—" he flashed that charmer grin "—I hope."

As if he didn't know, Elizabeth thought. The kid had everyone eating out of his hand.

"What I didn't realize until recently, is that all

those times I obeyed and studied, when I didn't understand why I should...I was learning more than Bible stories or Hebrew words. I was learning to accept adult responsibilities, to be proud of my Jewish heritage and committed to practicing Judaism the rest of my life.''

He turned and spoke to his parents as well as the congregation. ''That's what becoming a Bar Mitzvah means to me. And in a world without moral beliefs and obedience, or without great parents, I never would have had this learning experience. Thanks, Mom and Dad. I love you both very much.''

His huge ear-splitting smile marked the end of his speech. A collective swelling of pride filled the synagogue. Not a soul here, regardless of faith, didn't feel uplifted and hopeful about America's future—if young men like Ben were in it.

Elizabeth dabbed madly at her eyes as Rachel and Steven rose from their chairs, walked close to their son and stood side by side to face him. Rachel had been dreading this part, fearing she would be too choked up to speak. As of yesterday, Elizabeth knew, her friend hadn't been sure what she would say.

Steven dashed a thumb beneath one eye, then cleared his throat self-consciously. ''First of all, let me make it clear that occasionally, real men do cry.''

A few sympathetic masculine chuckles broke out. Elizabeth peered up at Cameron, who stared straight ahead, his eyes definitely a bit misty. She went all mushy inside.

"Ben, you are the mountain range of our lives. Your mother and I negotiate the peaks and valleys to the best of our ability. Sometimes smoothly, sometimes clumsily—but always with love and good intentions. Never forget that. You've worked very hard these past few months, and it shows. And I hope the sense of accomplishment you feel right now is as great as the pride I feel that you're my son."

Ben's young mouth trembled.

Elizabeth dabbed, dabbed, dabbed.

"You're no longer a little boy but a young man, with all the accompanying expectations and responsibilities of adulthood. But remember in the future, when you're pushed and pulled and confused, that your first and most important responsibility, is to respect and love yourself. It will make all your decisions clearer."

Steven looked at Rachel, who smiled tearfully and reached for his hand. Fingers threaded, they turned back to their son.

"Oy!" She laughed shakily, as did those who knew her well.

"My baby. Just look at you now. So tall and handsome. So much more a man than a boy. And not because of height, or a deep voice, or hitting home runs—or even the girls who call you on the phone. Those things may stroke a boy's ego…but they don't turn a boy into a man.''

She smiled tenderly at his blush, then grew solemn, her gaze holding the one so like her own. ''I have been so proud watching you learn to consider the consequences of your actions before you act. I have been so proud watching you learn that the world is a much bigger place than wherever you happen to be. I have been so proud—'' her voice grew husky, and dangerously wobbly ''—of watching you grow into a good…kind…responsible young man. And I have only one piece of advice for the future.''

Ben's eyes welled as she struggled to control her powerful emotion.

''If you ever,'' she said brokenly, ''have any doubt what a good, kind, responsible man would do in any situation…ask your father.'' She gazed up at her husband, her tears finally spilling free. ''He's the best man for the job.''

Steven obviously hadn't known what she was going to say, and looked deeply touched. Ben moved forward, and the three fell together in a fierce spontaneous hug.

Tissues were dabbing all over the synagogue. Elizabeth had resorted to her emergency backup, which was now a doughy wad in her fist.

Oh, this was what she wanted in her relationship with Cameron! Real, honest love, tested by honest life-changing challenges. Watching the tight family nucleus created by such a love, Elizabeth renewed her decision not to settle for anything less. To do so would ignore her first and most important responsibility.

To respect and love herself.

THE FOLLOWING THURSDAY, Cameron hunched over his calculator and busily entered data. All was quiet at Malloy Marketing. Everyone had left for home hours ago—including Elizabeth, with a box of personal belongings from the office she'd cleared for a new occupant.

He paused, hit the final button totaling his figures, then studied the digital readout for a long thoughtful moment.

Okay. It was a go.

Slumping back against his chair, he glanced at the stacked reports on his desk. A few numbers might change at the official end of the accounting period, but not enough to affect his decision.

Cameron waited for disappointment, or resentment, or the shame of failure to join his exhaustion—but experienced only a vague restlessness. Then a dawning realization.

Then wondering, wondrous relief.

His self-identity and happiness no longer revolved around Malloy Marketing. The world was a much bigger place than one small advertising agency striving to rise up the food chain in a big pond.

It had taken him nineteen years longer than Ben to learn that, Cameron thought wryly. But better late than never. And he desperately hoped Lizzy would agree.

In the week following the night they'd made love, he could've wooed her back into his arms. In her backyard she'd wanted him to kiss her, and God knew he'd wanted to do that and more. But Jake had helped Cameron see that his past history wouldn't repeat itself with Lizzy.

His six-date tolerance for other women didn't mean he was emotionally incapable of making a commitment. It only meant that none of those women had been the *right* woman. The one worth pushing himself to the limits for.

Knowing that what he felt for Lizzy was deep and abiding was one thing. Convincing her of that fact was another story. He'd decided the best way to earn her trust was to woo her properly, to show her she was special. Which meant he needed to keep physical chemistry out of the picture, and seduce her heart, instead of her body.

Funny how each selfless thing he'd done for her had enriched his own life and expanded his love tenfold.

He'd seen progress.

A hesitant hope behind her clear suspicion of his motives. She'd relaxed her guard a little more every day—until the Bar Mitzvah service Saturday morning.

Since then, he'd lost every bit of ground he'd gained, and she'd lifted shields he couldn't seem to penetrate. Not even the "L" word had broken through.

He hadn't meant to say it. Not like he had. Not when he had.

He'd wanted to "court" her gradually, with care and attention to what most touched her heart. He'd intended to plan a romantic sappy evening once she was well and truly ready to believe in his sincerity. Then he'd pop the question.

But when he'd seen her packing up her office earlier today and known she wouldn't return tomorrow, something inside him had snapped. He'd closed her door, told her he loved her and asked her not to leave—and instantly realized his mistake.

God, what an idiot! She'd thought his love for her was tied into her value to the agency. He'd seen it in her eyes, heard it in her polite refusal to stay. She'd gently requested that he put their relationship on hold so they could both review their feelings. Then she'd told him goodbye.

And he'd had the sickening impression she meant "Goodbye forever."

His gaze moved to the storyboards for TV commercials, print ad layouts, and key marketing points mounted on art boards leaning against the wall. The briefcase nearby held eight sixty-five-page marketing plans, custom-bound for each SkyHawk Airlines executive attending the three o'clock presentation tomorrow.

She'd fulfilled her obligation. He had no legal way to bind her to him.

From all appearances, he'd lost.

But he had one more ace up his sleeve.

He would lay down a final hand before accepting defeat. He would be playing for the biggest stake of his life, so he would play to win, according to her definition.

With everything he had, and no fear of what he might lose.

ELIZABETH POUNDED up Death Hill with grim determination, her feet as heavy as her heart.

She'd told Lucy last night how much fun they'd have today. They could sleep late, instead of getting up at dawn to jog. They could eat a leisurely breakfast, play a little fetch, watch a few soaps, maybe do a little shopping. PetsMart was having a great sale, and dogs were welcome in the store.

But Elizabeth had awakened at 5:00 a.m. as usual…then stayed stubbornly in bed for two more hours, just because she could. She'd scorched her pancakes, had overthrown a tennis ball into the neighbor's backyard kiddie pool filled with pea-soup water, remembered why she never watched soap operas even on vacation and had filled her basket at PetsMart only to discover at the checkout counter that she'd left her wallet at home in her black ''work'' purse. She'd grabbed her casual blue ''weekend'' purse out of habit. A natural mistake, given that she usually wore her gray sweat suit on weekends. She'd explained and apologized profusely.

But even so, she'd endured Lucy's accusing stare from the passenger seat all the way home.

At two o'clock, depressed and lethargic, she'd warded off an ice cream binge by tying on her good Nike trainers, snapping a leash on Lucy's collar and leaving the house. Exercise, Elizabeth had thought to herself. That was what she needed to lighten her mood. The sky was overcast, the breeze nippy, so she'd left her sweat suit on.

It was earning its name.

Jogging sucked. Her mood had gone from self-pitying to sour to downright surly by the time she'd reached Death Hill. She should've stayed inside and eaten Rocky Road ice cream. At least while she shoveled it into her mouth, her taste buds would've been happy. No part of her was happy now.

She hated sweating.

She hated this spawn-of-Satan activity called jogging.

She hated herself.

She hated everyone else more.

She hated loneliness.

She hated everything on the planet.

She hated everything in the solar system and all the known galaxies—

A tug on the leash jerked her gaze to bright dark eyes, flopping ears and a lolling tongue.

Okay. She didn't hate Lucy.

The admission opened a valve inside Elizabeth, releasing the petty steam driving her legs up to now. The initial gush weakened progressively in force until she crested the top of the hill, where it dissipated altogether. With the last of her energy, she passed the street lamp marking her finish line, slowed to a stop, leaned over and braced her hands on her knees.

She stared at the oil-stained cement, her breathing raspy but getting slower.

Lucy whined and strained against the leash.

"Wait," Elizabeth scolded. "I'm not in as good shape as you."

"I beg to differ," a deep voice said.

Her head snapped up. Her pulse drummed in her throat.

Cameron moved from behind Mrs. Doppler's

rose bushes and stepped into the street eight feet ahead. "Your shape is as good as it gets."

The leash jerked from Elizabeth's lax hand and Lucy bounded joyfully forward. He leaned over and fondled the retriever's adoring head, his gaze never wavering from Elizabeth's.

He wore jeans and a smoke-blue cableknit sweater. In the dreary light, his golden eyes were as warming as the sun.

She was suddenly conscious of baggy gray fleece and every hated trickle of sweat on her skin. "What are you doing here?"

Something akin to nervousness flickered in his eyes. He glanced down at Lucy and collected her leash. "You didn't answer the door. Lucy wasn't in the backyard. I thought you might've taken her for a walk or a run, and came looking."

His clothes registered. She checked her watch and gasped. "It's almost three! What are you doing here? Did the presentation get canceled? Have they rescheduled it yet?" She walked forward rapidly.

"Whoa, Nelly." He straightened. "One question at a time."

When she drew close, he began walking toward her house. Lucy padded calmly beside him on his left. Elizabeth fell into step on his right, near the curb.

"The presentation didn't get canceled," he said. "Or rescheduled."

"I don't understand. Is someone else taking your place?"

"No. Right about now, the SkyHawk Airlines conference room is filling up with eight executives, waiting for me to arrive."

"Then why are you here?" Alarm and confusion sharpened her voice.

"Because I had something better to do."

"Better?" She surged ahead of him. "Hurry! When we get to the house, I can call and make up some emergency. You were in a car accident. Your father had a heart attack. C'mon—" she spun around and walked backward "—help me out. You're the creative genius. Think."

He laughed hollowly. "That's all I've done for the past week, I assure you. This isn't a spontaneous decision."

Decision? Noting his strange expression, she slowed her steps and turned back around to walk beside him.

"Are you telling me you want to pull a no-show on Gary Matthews, without any call of explanation?"

"That's what I'm telling you."

"Cameron…" There were no words. "You'll lose the account," she said unnecessarily.

"I know."

Shock held her mute a long moment. "I don't understand."

His glance was hooded. "I know."

"But the agency... You need that account. Without it, you can't operate. What about Mitch and Susan and Tim and Pete and Joel? All their hard work on the presentation was for nothing? If the agency folds..." The ramifications clicked one upon another in her brain, like toppled dominoes. "My, God, *everyone* loses their job."

"Not necessarily. I'm going to offer Mitch and Susan joint ownership of the agency, if they want to assume the headaches and liabilities that come with it."

"What?"

"I've worked the numbers. If I take my salary and perks out of the overhead, the agency can break even for the next four months. That will give them time to bring in some new accounts."

She needed to sit down. The house was in sight, thank goodness. "Why would you give up your business?" Had he been diagnosed with a fatal disease? What? "Is there something you haven't told me?"

"Yes."

He stopped, which forced her to do the same. Dread clawed at her stomach.

"I haven't told you I want to drift off to sleep every night with you in my arms, and wake up every morning the same way."

Her lips parted in wonder.

"I haven't told you I want to cook you mushroom-cheese omelettes and share the newspaper with you and eat your mother's pot roast till I have to let out my belt."

Her heart fluttered against her ribs like a bird hitting a glass pane.

"I haven't told you I want daughters with curly black hair and big brown eyes, just like their beautiful mother, who is also smart and funny and wise and kind."

She pressed a hand between her breasts, against the ache of swelling emotion.

"I haven't told you I want a wife more than I want a vice president. Or that I want a soul mate more than I want Malloy Marketing."

Her head was buzzing. "You're giving up Malloy Marketing because you want me?"

"Want you, need you, adore you. I didn't know how else to make you understand how much I love you. Lizzy, I can find a job anywhere, doing anything. But you're one of a kind. I can't lose you. Marry me, Lizzy."

Her nose stung. Elizabeth swallowed hard. She felt exalted…and humbled…by his sacrifice.

He looked so earnest and worried, as if he actually thought he might lose her. She didn't tell him he'd won her before the mushroom omelette. It was too heavenly hearing him plead.

"I don't know, Cameron. I already said I

wouldn't marry you if you were the last man in Texas.''

His brows lowered. He slanted a look at Lucy.

"Sit," he ordered. Her haunches plopped down. "Stay," he added sternly.

He looked back at Elizabeth as if he'd like to order her to be as cooperative. "You didn't mean it."

"I'm so confused," she lied.

He stepped forward and thrust his hands above her ears. "Then let me make it simple."

His mouth came hungering.

She fed him gladly, with lips and teeth and tongue. Then took her own nourishment from his warmth and wetness. From his neediness. From his love.

He wrapped a powerful arm around her waist and pulled her against his thighs, letting her feel the truth of what she did to him. Raising his lips from hers, he said gruffly, "Say you'll marry me."

But before she could make a sound, his impatient mouth sought hers once more, and his tongue spoke messages her body pressed closer to receive. She hummed low in her throat, and he reared up his head.

"Say it," he demanded, his eyes burning.

"I'll marry you."

His nostrils flared. His eyes closed. He buried his

face in her neck and nearly cracked her ribs with his hug.

"On one condition," she said when she could breathe again.

He stiffened, then pulled back to look cautiously into her eyes. "What's that?"

"That you let me call Gary Matthews and tell him you were unavoidably detained but you'll be there in fifteen minutes." She was rewarded with a look so filled with love, she wondered if a person could die of happiness.

"You can call him on one condition," he said.

"Oh, yeah? What's that?"

"Tell him we'll be there. From now on, we do everything as a team."

SATURDAY NIGHT in the Mil Pescados Bar, three Ad Ventures employees were on their third round of margaritas when one of them said, "Psst! Don't look now, but Cameron Malloy just walked in the door."

Boos and hisses erupted.

"Who's the hot babe with him?"

"She's the one my source at SkyHawk told me about. The one who wore a sweat suit and charmed the old guy with some sappy story about a test of true love—somethin' like that, anyway. By the time they started their presentation, she had 'em all askin' for invitations to the wedding. Talk about sneaky gimmicks!''

''Yeah. I wish we'd thought of it.''

''Well, the last laugh's on Cameron. He never dates anyone very long. He'll lose the account the minute he dumps her, and we'll be waiting in the wings to step right in. Our campaign is ten times better than theirs.''

''I dunno. About the dumping, I mean. Are you looking at them?''

''Yeah, so...? Oh. Yeah, I see what you mean.''

''Hey, I heard that Sun States Airline is really unhappy with their agency.''

''No kidding?''

''My source says they gave ninety days' notice. First thing Monday, let's make a few calls.''

''Sounds like a plan.''

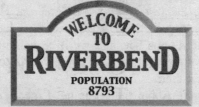

Your Romantic Books—find them at

www.eHarlequin.com

Visit the *Author's Alcove*

➣ Find the most complete information anywhere on your favorite author.

➣ Try your hand in the Writing Round Robin— contribute a chapter to an online book in the making.

Enter the *Reading Room*

➣ Experience an interactive novel—help determine the fate of a story being created now by one of your favorite authors.

➣ Join one of our reading groups and discuss your favorite book.

Drop into *Shop eHarlequin*

➣ Find the latest releases—read an excerpt or write a review for this month's Harlequin top sellers.

➣ Try out our amazing search feature—tell us your favorite theme, setting or time period and we'll find a book that's perfect for you.

All this and more available at

www.eHarlequin.com
on Women.com Networks

#924 BIRTHRIGHT • Judith Arnold
Riverbend

Aaron Mazerik is back. He isn't the town's bad boy anymore, but some people still don't think he's good enough—especially not for Riverbend's golden girl, Lily Holden. Which is fine with Aaron, since he's convinced there's even *more* reason he and Lily shouldn't be together.

Riverbend, Indiana: Home of the River Rats—small-town sons and daughters who've been friends since high school. These are their stories.

#925 FULL RECOVERY • Bobby Hutchinson
Emergency!

Spence Mathews, former RCMP officer and now handling security at St. Joe's Hospital, helps Dr. Joanne Duncan deliver a baby in the E.R. After the infant mysteriously disappears a few hours later, Spence and Joanne work closely together to solve the abduction and in the process recover the baby girl—and much more!

#926 MOM'S THE WORD • Roz Denny Fox
9 Months Later

Hayley Ryan is pregnant and alone. Her no-good ex—the baby's father—abandoned her for another woman; her beloved grandfather is dead, leaving her nothing but a mining claim in southern Arizona. Hayley is cast upon her own resources, trying to work the claim, worrying about herself and her baby.... And then rancher Zack Cooper shows up.

#927 THE REAL FATHER • Kathleen O'Brien
Twins

Ten years ago, Molly Lorring left Demery, South Carolina, with a secret. She was pregnant with Beau Forrest's baby, but Beau died in a car crash before he could marry her. For all that time, Beau's identical twin, Jackson, has carried his own secret. Beau *isn't* the father of Molly's baby....

#928 CONSEQUENCES • Margot Dalton
Crystal Creek

Principal Lucia Osborne knows the consequences of hiring cowboy Jim Whitely to teach the difficult seventh graders. Especially when Jim deliberately flouts the rules in order to help the kids. Certain members of the board may vote to fire Lucia and close the school. But Lucia has even graver consequences to worry about. She's falling in love with Jim...and she's expecting another man's child.

#929 THE BABY BARGAIN • Peggy Nicholson
Marriage of Inconvenience

Rafe Montana's sixteen-year-old daughter, Zoe, and Dana Kershaw's teenage son, Sean, have made a baby. *Now what?* Rafe's solution—or rather, proposal—has Zoe ecstatic, but it leaves Dana aghast and Sean confused. Even Rafe wonders whether he's out of his mind.